Simply Sexy

THE SIMPLY SERIES
BOOK 4

Carly Phillips

SIMPLY SEXY

It all started with a not-so-innocent sprig of mistletoe...

In retrospect, Rina Lowell should have known that Emma Montgomery's mistletoe was a matchmaking ploy.

Rina is new to Ashford, to her newspaper job, to her whole life. And she can't wait to write "Hot Stuff", a series of columns that will definitively pin down what men really want.

When Emma maneuvers her under that pesky sprig of evergreen with Ashford's prodigal son, Rina can't resist the chance to plant one on that dark-haired, blue-eyed man's sensual mouth. She never expected that kiss to go down like a shot of fine tequila. The man is perfect for her, or so she thinks.

When his adoptive father Joe falls ill, globetrotting news reporter Colin Lyons doesn't hesitate to drop everything to fly home and take over Joe's baby, the *Ashford Times*. Which, Colin discovers, is veering away from hard news to sexy, smutty fluff. Something he can't let happen.

He's only got until New Year's to save this sinking ship, and to do that, he needs an ally. Rina, with her sparkling brown eyes and frumpy clothes that make his fingers itch to discover what's underneath, is the perfect target to help him. Even if it means the job she loves will be cut in the end.

He never expected one kiss to take his simple plan to save the *Times* and tie it into impossible knots... and possibly cost him the woman he loves.

Prologue

EMMA MONTGOMERY STOOD by the window in the newspaper offices and tapped her manicured nails impatiently. Snowflakes told her Christmas was around the corner, and she adored the holiday, the cheer, the parties. She had no patience for imbeciles, a thought which reminded her to look back at the road. Still no sign of her driver. The man came and went on his own schedule. She wished she still had her license, but those days were gone. Thank goodness, she had other skills that hadn't dwindled with age. Matchmaking was her specialty and obviously, Corinne, the present publisher of the *Ashford Times,* had recognized her talent.

Emma was now the columnist for the *Ashford Times*'s "Meet and Greet" column, published in print and online. And she couldn't forget that this job had also saved her elegant behind from a nursing home. Her son, the Judge, had had it with her parties and antics, and if she didn't get busy with something, he'd threatened to put her in an senior living home.

She shivered, blaming the cold seeping in from the window. But the Judge's bellowing had done her a favor. She loved this job and the people here appreciated her talent and humor.

"Oh, Rina!" Emma called out to the only employee left in the office, the new girl named Rina Lowell.

Pretty name. Pretty woman. No makeup, but if Emma had that gorgeous skin, she wouldn't bother with blush, either.

Rina glanced up from her desk where she was typing away on her computer. "Yes, Emma?"

"You know that expression, all work and no play makes Rina an old fuddy-duddy?"

"I don't think you quite nailed it." Rina laughed, a light sound that would be musical to a man's ears. "Are you saying it's time I went home for the night?"

"Goodness, no!" Emma waved her hand in the air. "I'm saying we should hit the town and celebrate the new lives this news outlet has given us." Emma had been working for a few months and Rina had just recently started.

The young woman obviously wanted to make a good impression, arriving early and leaving late. But even the most dedicated worker had to have some fun.

"What did you have in mind?" Rina asked.

From the corner of her eye, Emma saw her car approach with her good-for-nothing driver, hired by her son, at the wheel. She might as well make use of his time and let him earn his money. "I thought we could go to O'Dooley's and have a beer."

Rina burst out laughing. "I'm sorry. I just can't picture you drinking beer."

"Phooey. You shouldn't make fun of an old lady. Would you prefer I have a shot of tequila?"

"I'll do one with you," Rina offered, her eyes twinkling with the challenge.

"You're on." Emma stuck out her hand for a shake. "At least I don't have to worry about drinking and driving. And if you come with me neither do you. Leave your car here. I'll drop you off at your home tonight and pick you up on the way to work tomorrow."

Rina pretended to give the idea some thought, but Emma caught the smile on her lips and knew the young woman had already decided.

Finally, she nodded. "Okay. I'm up for partying." She slid her chair back so she had room and pushed herself in a circle, hanging her head back and spinning the chair around before letting loose a loud whoop.

"What was that for?" Emma asked.

"I just wanted to act as free as I feel." Rina giggled. "I'm just *so* happy to have this job and so excited to start life over in Ashford."

Emma took in the young woman's pink flushed cheeks and wide smile. With her carefree attitude, she was the perfect candidate for Emma's matchmaking skills. She rubbed her palms, warming them together. "So, we're off to O'Dooley's."

"Do you think we'll meet any men t?" Rina asked as she pulled her purse out of the drawer in her desk. "Because with my new 'Hot Stuff' blog, I could use some good interaction."

Rina might claim her interest was in work, but Emma didn't miss the sparkle in Rina's gaze at the mention of meeting a member of the opposite sex. Oh, this was going to be fun, Emma thought. "With your cheekbones, you'd meet men anywhere."

"Why, thank you, Emma." Rina fluttered her mascara-free lashes with obvious exaggeration, then grabbed her winter coat from the back of her chair.

Emma wrapped her heavy shawl more securely around her shoulders. Together, they started for the door, but as they walked by the empty desk beside Rina's, Emma paused. "Can you believe the news?" she asked.

Rina shook her head. "I came in late today and worked all afternoon." She pointed to the earbuds she often wore when deep in thought. "What news?"

"The prodigal son has returned." Emma ran her hand over the old, empty desk. One no one was allowed to take in case Colin Lyons should return.

"I don't understand," Rina said.

"You already know that Corinne took over the paper from her sick husband, Joe."

The young woman nodded. "He's in the hospital and Corinne's worried."

"Right. And so is Joe's son. The man's a wanderer. He never stays in one place, to his poor father's chagrin." Emma placed a hand over her heart, knowing how she loved having her children and grandchildren around her. Even New York, where her granddaughter, Grace, lived, was too far away from Emma's home in Massachusetts. She couldn't imagine having a world traveler in the family. "But he's home now. And Corinne said he'll be working here." Emma pointed to the empty chair... a chair a few feet from Rina's desk.

The possibilities flitted through Emma's mind, giving her an adrenaline rush. Colin was a gorgeous man with sparkling blue eyes and the most amazing smile. But he'd never stick around for longer than he had to. Emma knew this because he'd been her grandson Logan's college roommate. She loved Colin like he was her own grandchild but felt he was missing out on so much that life had to offer. A warm bed to come home to, a good woman...

A woman like Rina.

Emma pursed her lips in thought. This was definitely something to consider. "Let's get going and I'll tell you all about Colin," Emma suggested.

"Sounds like a good plan." Rina headed out first, holding the door open for Emma. "Is he cute?" Rina asked.

"Gorgeous."

She raised an interested eyebrow. "Attached?"

Emma shook her head. "Completely free," she said and hoped she wasn't lying. She hadn't heard much about Colin's personal life lately. She'd have to ask Logan.

"Hmm."

"What does *hmm* mean?" Emma asked as she pressed the elevator button. She needed to know that Rina was open to a short-term relationship before she hooked her up with Colin. She'd never intentionally set anyone up for heartache, and though Emma would work toward something more permanent with these two, she couldn't be certain Colin would ever settle down.

Rina shrugged. "Just hmm." She tipped her head to the side. "You know, with this new job and new life, I can't help but think a little fun and excitement with a man ought to follow." She wriggled her eyebrows playfully. "You know what I mean."

Emma nodded. She certainly did. *Fun* meant something short-term. If Rina meant anything else, she would have chosen the word *relationship*. "You're horny."

"Emma!" Rina blushed a deep crimson. "You're terrible."

"I beg to differ. Holding back your thoughts is terrible. Speaking your mind is completely appropriate. Well, when among friends. And you are my friend." She put a hand on Rina's arm. "Something about you reminds me of my granddaughter, Grace. Or, at least, the way she was before I sent Ben to look after her. All this youthful exuberance and pent-up energy. All you need is the right man to let loose with." Emma nodded, certain she was correct.

"You think I'm horny, huh?" Rina laughed. "Believe whatever you want, but you're right about one thing. Letting loose is exactly what I have in mind."

Chapter One

One Month Later

"MARK MY WORDS, Joe. Sex will lead to the end of the world as we know it." Colin Lyons glanced at the hospital bed where his adoptive father and mentor lay sleeping.

Asleep, not dead. Thank God. After finding out Joe had had a stroke, Colin had hightailed it home from South America. He'd been covering a rigged election in a country where money laundering commingled with drug trafficking and guns blazed on the sunbaked streets. Now, one week later, Colin sat in the quiet hospital room watching the monitors prove to him Joe was alive. In the background, snow fell outside, a serene and peaceful reminder of winter. Of Christmas, of life, and hope.

Colin had taken leave from his job to come home and run Joe's beloved *Ashford Times* until the older man recovered, only to discover that he'd been usurped. Prior to his stroke, Joe hadn't been feeling well. Yet instead of calling on Colin, Joe had given his second wife, Corinne, power of attorney, which she'd used to almost run the newspaper—and Joe's legacy—into the ground. Colin's stomach cramped and twisted with guilt because he hadn't been around when Joe needed him. Worse, Joe hadn't thought his health was important enough to bother Colin with while he was on assignment.

He glanced toward the bed. A loud snoring sound reassured him that Joe wasn't down for the count. The doctors promised a full recovery, and he'd already begun the slow road toward recuperation. But time was something neither Colin nor the *Times* had on their side.

"Do you know that Corinne's turning the paper into a fluff-fest?" he asked, wondering if his words would penetrate Joe's sleepy fog.

They didn't. Joe's mouth opened wider in slumber as the clock on the wall ticked away the minutes of the day. Colin didn't mind. "There's a new blog on the online site called 'Meet and Greet: Matchmaking for the Aging but Still Sexually Inclined.'" Colin didn't expect a reply and wasn't surprised when he didn't get one.

He not only blamed Corinne for the beginning of the paper's change away from hard news but also for squandering the bank account, not keeping up with advertising, and her general lack of oversight. She'd brought the paper to the brink of bankruptcy, then foolishly thought she could fix things herself. Beginning by moving Emma Montgomery, a spunky senior citizen and his best friend's grandmother, from a desk job to a columnist.

He leaned back in his chair. "Emma means well but she takes this matchmaking thing too far. It's Christmas season, right? I had to stop her from hanging mistletoe and us getting slapped with a sexual harassment lawsuit."

Colin doubted Joe knew how bad the *Times*'s financial situation was, and telling him would only add stress and compromise his recovery. Besides, Colin already had things under temporary control.

He'd borrowed money from Ron Gold, an old friend of Joe's who believed, like Colin, that the paper had to return to the hard news that had made it a success to begin with. Based on a gentleman's handshake, Colin had promised to do everything in his power to shift things back.

Colin could handle working on Corinne to affect a change, but he needed time. Ron Gold understood. The paper's biggest advertiser didn't. They demanded Corinne's promise in writing to turn things around— focus on the news and get rid of the—in their opinion—"risqué" columns that now graced the front page and the main page online.

Otherwise, they threatened to pull their new ads scheduled for the first of the year, and the *Times* would lose its largest source of funding. Then even Ron Gold's loan wouldn't save them. Colin had until January 1. No longer. And he had no idea how to accomplish his goal with a woman who wouldn't listen to reason.

"Hello, Colin." Corinne breezed into the room, bringing with her the scent of heavy perfume. "How is he?" She walked over to the bed and stroked Joe's forehead.

Her gentle treatment of Joe didn't mesh with Colin's perception of her as being cold and self-absorbed. Then again, he hadn't been home often enough in the last couple of years to know her well. "He's sleeping."

She nodded and shrugged her jacket off her shoulders, revealing a low-cut, designer suit. Like the direction she was taking the paper, Corinne, her exposed cleavage and outward demeanor, oozed sex.

He glanced at his watch. Nearly three. "Long day at the office?" he asked.

"No, a fabulous one." Her eyes lit up as she spoke. "Wait until you read Rina's first column," she said of her newest addition to the *Ashford Times*'s staff.

Rina Lowell, a woman who Corinne had hired to write a weekly column with the heading "Hot Stuff."

A woman who intrigued him on many levels.

She had a creamy complexion and didn't bother

with makeup to enhance her image. He was fascinated by a female comfortable in her own skin. Her hair was pulled into a conservative bun he was dying to undo and see just how far the strands fell down her back. Her bare, naked back if he had his way. She possessed a husky voice with a New York accent she'd refined and hid her assets beneath bulky sweaters and baggy pants.

He had no idea what lay under the packaging but damned if he didn't want to find out. Hell, his fingers itched to strip off the thick layers and explore, inch by tantalizing inch.

Even with her eyes hidden by a pair of black-rimmed glasses, it was obvious that she thought and felt deeply. Rina got to him in a visceral sort of way and incited his journalistic blood, making him wonder what secrets she hid behind her intelligent brown eyes.

"Do you want a preview of what Rina has to say?" Corinne asked, breaking into his thoughts.

"Go ahead. I'm sure it'll be the highlight of my day."

"It's simply sexy," she replied, either missing or ignoring his sarcasm.

Her excitement over her new employee was almost tangible, reminding him of why he needed to steer clear of Rina Lowell. She sided with the opposition and contributed to the fluff Corinne still seemed to think would sell papers.

That alone put Rina off-limits. "What's simply sexy?" he forced himself to ask. "Rina's column?"

"No, the title of her series of articles is *Simply Sexy*." Corinne shook her hair, deliberately letting her blond mane flow over her shoulders. "Simply fabulous if you ask me. She's going to bring in a whole new set of readers." She still sounded so certain despite her track record of mistakes in the past few months.

He shook his head, amazed reality hadn't set in. She hadn't conceded defeat, not even when forced to accept Colin's check to keep the paper afloat for an extended period of time.

"Corinne, people subscribe for one reason. To read the news." He figured he'd try one more time to make his point.

"The news is everywhere. Television, radio, even on people's computer screens. They can buy the *Boston Globe* for news. I want to give them something different." She waved her hand for emphasis, and her gold bracelets clinked together.

Surprisingly, Joe didn't react. It was a noise he must be used to hearing in his sleep.

"I admit I started off slow and on the wrong foot, but with Rina and Emma on board, I'm getting there. People may be resistant to change, but that doesn't mean I can't win them over," Corinne insisted.

Colin groaned, resigned to the inevitable. She wasn't ready to cave in yet. But no matter how hard Corinne tried, sex wouldn't sell newspapers.

It wasn't that Colin had anything against sex. Hell, he was a man, wasn't he? But sex had its time and place. And it had been sadly lacking in his life, he silently admitted. The dry spell had gone on too long. Still, he wasn't about to embark on a meaningless fling. Casual sex was neither smart nor satisfying, and travel didn't lend itself toward establishing long-term relationships.

Apparently, neither did sticking around. His marriage had bottomed out fast because his wife didn't know the meaning of fidelity. She'd cheated on Colin. Twice. Two different men, Lord knew how many times with each. Colin had left town soon after the discovery. Sick of the reminder of past failure, he'd booked a flight to Europe, trading in a local TV anchor job for one abroad.

"I'm going to make sure Joe's doctor knows to stop by and talk to me before he leaves the hospital tonight," Corinne said as she walked toward the door.

"That's fine. I'll stick around until you get back." He wanted the older man to know he had people by his side and a family to return to when he walked out of the hospital even if Colin wasn't sure Joe knew that anyone was in the room.

Corinne disappeared out the door just as Joe's snoring became obscene. Colin grinned, the sound calming him in ways only his heart understood. Joe and his first wife, Nell, had taken Colin in when his parents died. At twelve, he'd been a pain-in-the-ass kid who thought he knew best and resented the world because his parents were gone. But Joe and Nell understood. They gave him time, space, and a home in which to adjust. Later on, they'd adopted him, even knowing he couldn't bring himself to call anyone but his birth parents Mom and Dad. They'd just wanted him to feel loved and know he had family. The same thing Colin wanted for Joe now. Which was why he forced himself to get along with Corinne even if he wanted to throttle her.

Joe's snoring continued and Colin laughed. When Joe wasn't at work, he'd always spent a great deal of time snoring in his old recliner chair. A chair Corinne had dragged to the street corner the day she'd said, "I do." Colin didn't know what possessed Joe to marry a woman the complete opposite of Nell. But he had.

"I'm back." Corinne carried two soda cans in her hand. "I brought you a cola."

Again, Colin was struck by the incongruity of her actions. "Thanks," he muttered. Obviously, Joe had seen something in her, which was another reason Colin wanted to give her a chance.

Just not where Joe's beloved paper was concerned.

"When you get back to the office, take a look at Rina's column. I promise you'll be impressed," Corinne said, taking his place in the chair by Joe's bed.

Colin forced a nod. But at the reminder of what he had waiting for him, he snorted in disgust. Matchmaking ads, self-help articles, and a series on what men want? He was beginning to doubt either Corinne, Rina Lowell, or any other woman had a clue.

He let himself out of the hospital room and leaned against the back wall next to a utility cart. Corinne had already told him she didn't believe their advertiser would pull their new ads, not once they saw how readers reacted to Rina's first column and the other assorted new things she had planned. Reality wasn't a part of Corinne's thinking, and Colin's frustration flew as fast and furious as his thoughts.

Corinne was so caught up in her newest scheme she didn't care or understand that her livelihood and Joe's legacy were at stake. How the hell could he reach her? She was so damn excited about Rina's new series she wouldn't listen to reason.

He ran a hand through his hair. And the solution dawned.

Rina. Corinne's newest flavor of the week. An employee she obviously trusted. Someone with whom he'd heard Corinne shared a family connection. A bond. Rina Lowell might be the only person who could make Corinne see the error of her ways. *If* Colin could get Rina on his side.

He'd have to spend time with her in order to subtly sway her to his way of thinking. Considering she'd piqued his interest from day one, being with Rina would be no hardship. But gaining her trust under false pretenses didn't sit well with him, and guilt gnawed at his insides. He'd be pursuing friendship, all the while knowing he was plotting a return to hard news at the expense of her job.

He attempted to assuage his guilt with the facts. Rina would be out of a job whether Corinne ran the paper into the ground or Colin got things back on track. But if he got to know her first, if she believed he wanted what was best for all involved, maybe she'd be willing to help him talk Corinne into accepting the best of all possibilities. They could save the paper, and in return, he could promise Rina a good recommendation for another, more appropriate job.

He groaned, still feeling like a shit for considering the plan. But feelings didn't change the fact that the *Times* was a newspaper, not a woman's magazine, something the advertisers—and now Colin's lender—understood. The money he'd contributed would only hold out for so long. They needed positive cash flow again soon.

A smart man would hop on the next plane back to South America. But Colin couldn't. Not yet. Financial debt and gentleman's agreement aside, Colin had more compelling reasons to stay. He hadn't been here when Joe first got sick, and Colin lived with that knowledge every damn day. He loved, respected, and owed the man. Joe had given him a shot in life, and Colin wouldn't betray him now.

Colin wouldn't allow anyone to destroy the paper Joe had built. He'd do anything he had to for the older man. Even if it meant using Rina Lowell.

RINA WATCHED WITH amusement as the head of the maintenance crew tried to hang mistletoe according to Emma Montgomery's direction. The older woman had already hung sprigs in unsuspecting places around the *Ashford Times*'s offices and had taken to adding a bit more each day. Of course, she did her decorating after five, when the core staff had gone home for the day.

"A little more to the left. No, to the right. Left. No, right." From her seat, Emma tried to choreograph everything and everyone in her sphere of influence, a mean feat for an eighty-year-old woman. At least, Rina thought she was eighty. Emma never discussed her actual age.

"Geez, lady, make up your mind." The man's

weight tipped the ladder precariously with each stretch of his arm in a different direction. "I haven't got all night."

Emma sniffed. "That's the problem with today's generation. Everyone's in such a rush. What do you think, Rina? Come here and check it out from my perspective."

Knowing Emma wouldn't be satisfied unless she complied, Rina shut down her computer for the night and joined the older woman. She glanced upward at the ceiling. "Looks good to me. Want to test it out? Emma's willing," Rina jokingly told the maintenance man.

He glared, obviously not enjoying his role in holiday merrymaking.

Emma laughed. "You need holiday spirit," she informed the man, then squinted upward once more. She nodded at last. "That's it then. Leave the mistletoe there."

Directly over Colin Lyons's chair. Despite Corinne's warning, his return had shocked the staff. Those who knew Colin had expected his long absences to continue. Instead, as soon as he'd arrived home, he'd come on board at the paper. Corinne had agreed to let him take over the small news department, admitting that wasn't her forte. But even she didn't think he'd stay. According to office gossip, he never did.

Rina glanced at the greenery over his seat and grinned. "You are one wicked woman, Emma."

She rubbed her hands together with glee. "Tell me you wouldn't love to get that man underneath the mistletoe."

Of course, she would. But Rina wouldn't be admitting anything to Emma. No way would she give the queen of the "Meet and Greet" column a cause to focus on. She could handle her own affairs, thank you very much. Because if Emma discovered that Rina was attracted to Colin—incredibly attracted, in fact—she'd pull out all the stops to get them together. And the timing was all wrong for Rina to find herself on the receiving end of Emma's renowned matchmaking skills.

With her series coming up, she had put together a plan to decipher what the opposite sex wanted. She couldn't have Emma meddling in her social life. Not now.

Even if Colin did light megawatts of electricity inside her every time he walked into the room. Those arresting blue eyes, that thick black hair, his distinctive masculine scent all set off heavy-duty sparks of desire. Instant sexual attraction, she thought. And female intuition, plus the fact that she'd often caught him staring, told her he felt the chemistry between them, too.

Emma narrowed her gaze. "Silence is an answer in itself." She patted Rina's arm, rose, and headed slowly back to her own desk.

"Come on, Emma. Pick on someone your own age," Rina said.

The older woman laughed. "You're a challenge, Rina. I thrive on challenges and I live to matchmake. What exactly do you live for, dear?"

"Until lately, not much," she admitted. After her husband's death, guilt had consumed her. He'd been rushing home from a business trip in the pouring rain, coming to be with her instead of sensibly spending the night at a hotel.

For a long while after, Rina hadn't thought life had much to offer. But after some soul-searching, she sold the New York City penthouse she and her husband had shared and decided it was time to live again. Financially secure and free to do whatever she wanted, Rina had had no desire to return to her job as a legal secretary. It had been a decent means of earning a living, but it didn't satisfy her.

She'd asked herself what would, looking inside herself for answers. She'd always been curious about human nature, drawn to people and relationships. Like Emma, she'd even indulged in matchmaking with her brother, Jake, and his wife, Brianne. She'd decided to use her people skills and her childhood habit of writing and documenting ideas and put them to good use.

And now, she had her column. "But my outlook is fresh and new since moving to Ashford," she said, meaning every word.

Emma nodded. "Good thing you packed up and moved on." She studied Rina with eyes full of wisdom.

"Amen, sister." Rina grinned and hit Emma's hand in a high five, laughing at the older woman's spunk.

Rina had no doubt Emma had seen a lot in the decades she'd lived, and she'd obviously learned how to get the most out of every person she met and opportunity she saw, a philosophy Rina had adopted, too, from the minute she'd decided to sell the penthouse and move on. So what if she'd had to pull a few strings to get this job?

Corinne's father lived in the same retirement community as Rina's parents. Of course, Corinne's father was much older than Rina's parents, but in Florida, if a man had teeth and the ability to walk upright, golfing and bridge buddies formed. When Rina learned that Corinne had taken over her husband's newspaper, she picked up the phone, the two women hit it off, and Rina had herself a job. One she wouldn't hold on to if she wasn't successful.

But she would be.

"Ah. More silence. You're thinking. That's okay. As long as you speak wisely to yourself, that's what counts." Emma broke into Rina's musings. "But if you should want to share your thoughts, I'd be more than happy to listen."

"You're so nosy." Rina glanced at Emma with all the warmth she felt toward her. "Not to mention perceptive."

"Live as long as I have and you'd better have learned something," Emma replied with a wink. "Now, I want to hear more about your upcoming series. Did I mention that I admire your gumption?"

"Not lately," Rina said wryly.

Ignoring the writing implement tucked behind her ear, Emma picked up a pencil and tapped the eraser against the desk. "Catching a man is so much more complicated today than in my youth. Instead of pinching cheeks for color, you swipe on blush, and in place of tissues, implants are all the rage now." She paused for an obvious inspection of Rina's attributes.

Rina shook her head. The older woman was unbelievable.

"What do men want? Pfft," Emma said. "You'll never know because they'll never tell." She waved a regal hand in the air, dismissing the notion out of hand.

"I don't want them to tell me, I plan to use my

powers of observation to figure it out. Methodically." Rina pulled out her phone and glanced at the list she'd compiled in her Notes. "And it's not just appearance. It's also in how a woman acts, walks, and talks." She swiveled her hips for effect.

"More movement," Emma suggested.

Rina sashayed her waist and ended with a rendition of Britney Spears that would do any twenty-year-old proud. From across the room, one of the remaining layout editors who was just putting on his jacket applauded.

Rina grinned and bowed. "You see? Attitude makes a difference," she said with a nod. "The question is what's more important? Attitude or intellect? Wouldn't a smart man want a woman with whom he can carry on a breakfast conversation?" she asked Emma.

"No. Men want arm candy."

Rina cocked her head to the side. "Come on. They can't all be that shallow a species."

Emma rolled her eyes. "Get with the program, Rina. All men want a woman they're proud to display on their arm. It's the male ego, dear."

"That's true." Much as she hated to admit it. Take her deceased husband. After their marriage, he'd ostensibly fired her as his legal secretary, giving her a life of luxury most women would love. In exchange, he'd wanted a stay-at-home wife, one who was comfortable entertaining guests and who dressed well so he was proud to have her by his side. "You do have a point."

"And trust me," Emma said. "The reason you're still flying solo after being in this town for three months is because you're doing nothing to enhance your appearance."

Rina put a hand to her unflattering bun and grinned. "I know."

"Forgive me, but I simply don't understand." Emma shook her head, her look of confusion obvious. "I can see your potential. I've offered to have my limo driver take us to Bloomingdale's for a clothing makeover, offered to have my stylist come do your hair. You refuse. Care to tell me why?"

"Corinne hired me to bring life to the paper with my series idea. I can only do that by giving my readers personal experience. So, I started by establishing myself in town as a quiet, inconspicuous woman."

Emma pursed her lips. "Go on."

"I've been researching from day one here. Recording men's reactions to this Rina." There hadn't been much attention paid to the woman who wore baggy clothes and no makeup, one who possessed a mild-mannered personality. Although Colin's heated gaze more than made up for the other men's lapses. "So, now I'm going to alter my appearance and actions and see what kind of changes men react to. So I can impart firsthand wisdom to my readers."

"You're going to strut your stuff." Emma grinned. "I like that."

"You would."

"Can I help it if I've got my finger on the pulse of male-female relationships? Why, just look at Logan and Cat," she said, referring to her wealthy grandson and his beloved wife.

Rina knew Emma credited herself with that pairing.

"Then there's Grace and Ben. If only they didn't live in New York," Emma said wistfully. "You'll meet Logan and Cat at the Christmas party Saturday night, but you'll have to look up Grace next time you return to New York for a visit."

The older woman also took responsibility for her granddaughter Grace's marriage to the detective Emma had hired to look out for her in New York City. Rina suspected that both of her grandchildren would have succeeded without their grandmother's help, though Rina had to admit they wouldn't have met without Emma's meddling.

"So, we're talking a random sampling of men?" Emma asked.

Rina nodded. "Anyone and everyone, including the

deliveryman. And the pizza guy is particularly cute." Not that he'd been attracted to Rina and her plain, unflirtatious side, but the time had come to change her attitude. Because not only was this series her journalistic debut, but it also marked her return to the social scene.

She was ready to begin flirting again, testing her wiles on the opposite sex. The best part was that she'd been able to use her daily life as research since she met men at the coffee shop next door and at the bar favored by her downstairs neighbor, Francesca— Frankie, for short. They both rented apartments in a Cape house Rina had heard about from Corinne. One look and Rina had fallen in love with the house and made friends with Frankie, whose favorite pastime was discussing dating in Boston. They shared information, and Rina's ideas flourished. She'd already outlined her series and written most of the first week's draft.

With work put aside, she could focus on her private life. And Emma had been right on when she'd called Rina horny. She hadn't been with a man in years, and she was finally open to the concept of monogamous sex. She wasn't ready for a relationship, but a satisfying fling appealed to her new independent streak and resolve to live life on her own terms.

"Any ideas who should be your first guinea pig?" Emma asked, obviously referring to Rina's column.

Rina, on the other hand, contemplated what kind of man she'd like in her bed. "A dark-haired, blue-eyed Mr. Perfect," she said dreamily. An attentive man who catered to her every need and desire.

"Afternoon, ladies." As if she'd conjured him, dark-haired, blue-eyed Colin Lyons appeared near where Rina stood. She hadn't noticed him come in, but she was very aware of him now.

She inhaled and smelled the musky scent of his cologne and her stomach curled with delicious warmth. She told herself it had to be the thought of sex that had her hot and bothered, but she knew she lied. Just looking at Colin elicited a definite chemical reaction inside her body, obviously short-circuiting her brain.

"Hello, Colin. I take it you were at the hospital again?" Emma asked, knowing Colin had visited Joe every afternoon since his arrival the day of the publisher's stroke.

Colin nodded.

"How is our dear Joseph?" Emma asked.

"Resting more comfortably today."

"That's wonderful. I know Corinne's worried about him," Rina added, joining the conversation and trying to act polite, not like the oversexed female he inspired her to be.

"Corinne's got a lot to be worried about," he muttered, then turned to Rina. "But I appreciate you asking. I'll be sure to tell Joe you care," he said, his voice warm.

As usual, his attention set off a tingling reaction. "Emma asked about Joe first," she reminded him, trying to deflect attention from herself. Surely, Joe would rather hear about Emma's concern than an employee he hadn't even met.

"She did. But so did you, and as Joe's family, I appreciate it." A smile tilted Colin's lips into a lopsided grin, and Rina forgot to breathe.

A former local newscaster, he had the chiseled features television adored, dimples, and a gleaming white smile made more charming by the slight overlap of his two front teeth. Razor stubble darkened his cheeks, and that hint of musky aftershave enhanced his potent allure. Her gaze traveled downward. Even his fisherman sweater and worn jeans added to his rugged appeal.

"See something you like?" he asked, arms folded across his broad chest.

"Everything," she said, immediately biting her tongue, but it was too late. The word had escaped.

Caught, she flushed and quickly transferred her gaze to Emma. Rina tried to look innocent. She really did. But when Emma nodded Colin's way and murmured, "I agree, he's hot, but put your tongue back in your mouth," the slight flush in Rina's cheeks started to burn.

"You'll have to forgive Rina. She's off-balance," Emma said to Colin. "And I can't really blame her, considering." She propped an elbow on her desk.

"Considering what?" Colin spoke to Emma, but his blue-eyed gaze never left Rina's. He hadn't stopped staring since her blunt admission.

Emma sighed. "Young people. You never take time to look around you and appreciate the scenery."

Oh, if Emma only knew how wrong she was, Rina thought wryly, realizing Colin's eyes had small laugh lines surrounding them, a sexy attribute that added character to an already amazing face.

"Look up, children. You're both standing under mistletoe," Emma said with glee. With a huge smile on her face, Emma pointed up.

Rina groaned, and Colin, one eyebrow raised, followed Emma's lead to look at the ceiling. Sure enough, the green sprig hadn't moved, changed, or fallen to the floor. And neither had Rina since the time Emma had called her over to Colin's desk.

She'd been had. A notion the older woman verified when she not so subtly picked up her purse.

"Well, Colin?" Emma asked. "Aren't you going to follow tradition?"

Rina knew from experience life rarely doled out

second chances. Standing under the mistletoe with Colin was a one-time opportunity. She'd been doing a lot of talk about living a new life and starting over. True, she was in the office but she didn't feel there was any pressure on either side.

She glanced up at the mistletoe that teased her and tempted her to follow her most erotic impulses. Emma had obviously caught the sexual undercurrents that had been running between Rina and Colin since day one.

No sense trying to hide them now.

"I wonder," she whispered softly, for Colin's ears only. Taking advantage of the new, liberated Rina, she leaned forward, closer to Colin and those super-sexy lips. "Do you have the nerve?"

Chapter Two

FROM THE CORNER of her eye, Rina saw Emma slip out the door.

"Emma's gone," Colin said. He sounded as stunned as she felt at this sudden turn of events, and his voice held a husky, low timbre that resembled rough whiskey.

"And she definitely left some excitement in her wake."

"Is that what you'd call it?" He studied her shamelessly as if taking her measure. Looking for what Rina couldn't be sure, but with each passing second, those blue eyes seemed to see inside her.

To read her mind. If he could, he'd know she took this tradition seriously. Now that Emma had put the idea in her mind, she wanted to know what it would feel like to be kissed under the mistletoe. Right now. By Colin.

His hands came to rest on her shoulders, his palms hot and strong. Heat burned within her and her stomach curled with silken anticipation as the need to taste him grew.

"Rina?"

"Yes?"

He removed her glasses, placing them on the desk, and stared. "Did you know you have golden flecks in those brown eyes?"

Unable to speak, she licked her dry lips and was rewarded when his hungry gaze followed the movement.

"Reminds me of sunshine."

Warmth tingled through her veins. Born and raised in the Bronx and a New York girl at heart, Rina wasn't shy about asking for what she wanted. And she wanted her new life to begin now. Despite barely knowing Colin, she was going to test the waters. Take whatever he was willing to give. "You should know I'm not one to let a mistletoe moment pass."

"And you should know I'm not a man who takes a challenge lightly," he said, obviously referring to her earlier question. Did he have the nerve to kiss her? "However, I'm not up for a sexual harassment lawsuit from an employee."

She respected that. "But I asked you." She raised an eyebrow, challenge continuing.

"Then far be it for me to defy tradition. No matter how unexpected," he whispered an instant before he lowered his head and his lips touched hers.

He'd called her bluff, taken the initiative, and now he toyed with her, playfully testing, learning the feel of her mouth, and letting her discover him. Then his tongue slid briefly, seductively, over the seam of her lips, electrifying her with his touch until their tongues lightly met.

The experiment yielded high-impact results. Colin tasted of pure male desire, a flavor that stirred a hunger long-denied and awakened passions she'd never experienced before. Passions she'd never thought existed before now. She trembled, and in response he squeezed her shoulders, his fingers biting into her skin, providing a carnal awareness of the fact that she affected him, too.

But from deep inside, caution clawed its way to the surface, breaking through the surprising desire that still burned hot inside her. She'd been floored by a simple kiss.

As if anything about this kiss—or Colin—was simple.

She lifted her head, breaking the kiss but not the awareness. He met her gaze. Heat flared bright in his eyes and flushed his cheeks, and the shock that reverberated inside her was evident in his expression. Another emotion shared.

She stepped back and ran trembling fingers over her lips. "That was…"

"Fun."

Not exactly the word she'd have chosen, and Rina

blinked, startled.

"Isn't that what kissing under the mistletoe is supposed to be?" Colin shot her a boyish grin.

She wished it was as easy for her. She exhaled hard and forced a casual smile before meeting his eyes. "Of course, it was fun. Emma set us up and we responded like any two adults caught under the mistletoe would."

She took a step backward, then another. A few more and she made it to her desk so she could regroup, leaving Colin alone under the mistletoe laden with tradition.

"Fun's meant to be repeated." His expression still showed shocked surprise, but he couldn't hide the warm appreciation in his gaze.

She reached for her jacket, caught off-guard when he stepped forward and helped her slip on her wool coat. His hands were gentle as he adjusted her collar, and his calloused fingers brushed her nape, eliciting a tingling sensation that shot straight to her toes.

She hadn't known he was a gentleman. "Thanks."

"My pleasure."

Without turning, unwilling to look into those blue eyes once more, she barely managed to grab her series folder, call a quick goodbye, and beat a hasty retreat to the door.

"Rina, wait."

She turned, her heart pounding hard in her chest.

"What?"

"You forgot something."

She accepted her glasses and bolted into the cold night.

As the icy whip of wind hit her cheeks, it was easier to think clearly. With that kiss, her experiment had taken on even more exciting, somewhat illicit overtones.

She still planned to experiment for her column. Starting tomorrow, she'd test out men as a group in general. But when it came to Colin, she was fully aware of his impact. With a single kiss, she'd learned he wielded power. Sexual, seductive power, and she found that lure thrilling.

Before tonight, she'd merely toyed with the notion of a fling, but now the idea of an affair took on real possibilities. Colin possessed enough sex appeal to light Rina's fire. He also used jet fuel to propel his frequent departures. Colin wasn't a stick-around sort of guy. If she were looking for a future, he'd be the last man on her list. But after losing her husband, she was wary of a long-term relationship and was no longer sure she believed in forever. Which made a fling the perfect solution.

And Colin the perfect man.

COLIN KICKED BACK, propped his feet on the desk, and watched the door slam closed behind Rina Lowell, the woman he'd just kissed under the mistletoe.

He'd been given an unexpected opportunity, and being human—as well as damned attracted to Rina— he'd kissed her. He shouldn't have. Through Rina, Colin hoped to understand how to get through to Corinne, but he'd never intended to take advantage. Especially since he held her career in his hands. True, she'd not only started it but assured him he wasn't taking advantage, but it hadn't been smart. For many reasons.

Getting involved with Rina would tear at his loyalties, though he had no doubt who would win. Colin had let Joe down once before. He refused to do it again, so Joe and his paper had to come first. Yet the paper had been the last thing on his mind when he'd had Rina in his arms.

And now, he was in deep. Because he hadn't counted on being completely seduced. And from the moment he'd opened the doors to the office and seen Rina shaking her hips and shimmying her body, he *had* been. Enough to make him watch like a damn voyeur as she'd continued her conversation with Emma. She'd called out to him, luring him in, and by the time he'd walked over to the desk, he'd been entranced by her combination of natural beauty and erotic movement.

He couldn't delude himself into thinking he'd imagined the combustion they'd created together. The heat. The texture. The intensity. The unexpected *connection*. She'd felt it too or else she wouldn't have run far and fast.

He rubbed his hands against his jeans and groaned. In the aftermath, she'd stared at him warily, shock in those huge brown eyes. She didn't know what to make of him.

Unexpectedly, that bothered him.

Guilt nudged at him again, stronger now when he contemplated his need to dethrone Corinne and her new entourage of employees. He *liked* Emma. And Rina... Well, he'd more than enjoyed her. His gut told him not to mix business with pleasure, and everything about Rina screamed pleasure.

But Colin was a man cornered by necessity and all out of options, save one. A gorgeous brunette named Rina Lowell.

THIS WASN'T RINA'S first day of work, but excitement rushed through her veins. She was on a dual mission today, beginning her experiment at work and laying the groundwork for seducing Colin. She tried to swallow but her mouth had grown dry.

The day started like any other. Her first stop was

the coffee shop downstairs from the office. Because Ashford was a wealthy oceanside community, the café was an upscale place offering a variety of designer drinks. The owner, a good-looking man in his mid-thirties, greeted everyone with the same compulsory smile. Rina had made many conversational openings in the past, but he'd never reacted or picked up on any of them. Yet she'd heard through the building grapevine that the more attractive women were offered an extra shot of caramel or mocha in their lattes, free of charge. Plain Rina had always paid for hers.

She'd only worked on some subtle physical changes today as she was saving the big guns for the Christmas party over the weekend. She didn't expect any special treatment just yet, but she intended to find out if makeup, even light brushes of color and hue, made a difference in how men treated women. And she planned to impart that wisdom in her next column.

"Next." The man wiped down the counter and glanced at Rina. "What can I get for you?"

Coffee, tea, or me sounded too clichéd, so she opted for a straightforward, "Whatever you do best will suit me just fine." She tipped her head, letting her ponytail hang down over her shoulder. Same head-tip she'd given him when she'd worn her plain old bun. But today, it was no coincidence that her hair dangled just over one breast.

He leaned down on one elbow, getting closer and meeting her gaze. Up close, he was too pretty for Rina's taste. She preferred a dark-haired, masculine man whose kiss lingered and who'd starred in her late-night fantasies. At the thought of Colin, she could have purred out loud.

"Dave's special is chocolate malted cappuccino," he said with a ridiculous abundance of pride.

"Which means you're Dave." Rina forced a welcoming, wide smile for a man who did nothing for her. "Make mine with extra chocolate and you've got yourself a deal."

Five minutes later, she walked back onto the snow-covered street with an extra-large chocolate malted cappuccino for the price of a regular-size latte in one hand, a black coffee in the other, and a date request for Saturday night. Thank God she'd had Emma's Christmas party as an excuse to decline.

Score one for men being visual animals, Rina thought. Dave had reacted to her looks, or maybe it was the hair. He'd hit on her today when he hadn't given her a second glance yesterday. In this case, chemistry didn't matter as much as superficial impressions. If she had a free hand, she'd jot notes on her phone. She decided she'd handle it upstairs. Rina had no doubt she wouldn't forget details about this particular outing.

She turned and headed inside her office building. Rina knew most employees' schedules as well as she knew her own. Colin tended to arrive early in time to get Marty's freshly made coffee before it'd had a chance to gel and petrify. She strode through the office, a room comprising desks, computers, and an occasional portable divider for the more senior editors. And she immediately noticed that Colin was already in his chair but he didn't have a mug in front of him. Yet.

Instead, he sat flipping through mail and muttering to himself. Even aggravated, the man was so damned sexy. It wasn't just the black leather jacket that hung on his chair, though it added to his rugged appeal. And it wasn't his windblown hair or the intelligence lurking in his blue eyes. His allure came from somewhere deeper, somewhere inside him. Intensity defined Colin Lyons and every move he made.

She paused a moment, gathering her courage, and when she bit down on her lip, she tasted lipstick, a reminder of today's changes. Like Dave, she expected Colin to notice and react. Her heart rate picked up rhythm at the prospect. Taking the coffee she'd purchased, she strode to his desk, coming up beside him.

He leaned back and glanced toward the corner, oblivious to her presence. "How is it I barely recognize this place?" he asked himself.

His dark tone didn't bode well for her plan to dazzle him. Taken with the depth of his feelings, she felt an unexpected tug at her heart. She glanced around, wanting to view things from his perspective and see just what was upsetting him. Mistletoe still hung from the ceiling and a gorgeous tree stood in the corner adorned with gold and silver tinsel and exquisite decorations.

Yet despite the holiday cheer, he'd sounded distressed.

"That sounded depressing. Do you have something against Christmas?" she asked.

"Against the holiday? No. Against the tree? Hell, yes." He didn't turn to face her.

As someone who'd grown up with handmade ornaments, then progressed to the expensive, exclusive store-bought kind when she married, Rina recognized Corinne's tree as the latter version. That obviously bothered Colin, though Rina couldn't imagine why.

Despite all the reasons not to get emotionally involved, she wanted to know what he was feeling and why he was feeling it. "What do you have against some poor defenseless tree?"

"That corner is usually reserved for Joe's hand-cut pine." Colin's voice held a hint of gruffness combined with tender emotion.

And this poor tree had obviously replaced Joe's. "I'm sure Corinne meant well. Maybe she thought some tree was better than no tree," Rina offered, trying to soothe the sting he suffered.

"Corinne didn't mean anything except satisfying her own personal need to spend."

It was the first time she'd heard him attack Corinne, and the shock rattled her. Though she didn't know the other woman well, Rina had always been a decent judge of character, and Corinne seemed to genuinely care about people in general, her employees and especially her sick husband.

He shook his head. "Never mind. I didn't mean that the way it came out."

"Maybe not, but something's bothering you. Whatever it is, you need to get it out."

"And you want to hear?" He sounded surprised.

Was it so shocking that she wanted to help him? They were strangers, but the holidays often brought unexpected people together, and the mistletoe *had* begun their journey.

She nodded, then, realizing he couldn't see her, she answered with a soft, "Yes. I'd very much like to hear."

He leaned back in his seat. Silence reigned. Maybe he was considering whether he wanted to share.

"We had a yearly tradition, Joe and I," he said at

last.

Rina released the breath she hadn't been aware of holding.

"It started the year Joe and his first wife, Nell, took me in after my parents died in a car accident. I was twelve at the time."

Having grown up with both parents and having lived a decent family life, her heart squeezed tight at the admission that he'd lost his parents young. Family was important to Rina and she found herself glad that Colin had had Joe and Nell to compensate for his loss. "I didn't know."

"No reason you should. Joe and Nell ended up adopting me. And since it's part of Joe's earlier life, it's probably not something Corinne likes to discuss."

Rina doubted that, but Colin obviously had issues with his adoptive father's young wife. It was the story of many families, so she chose to listen rather than defend Corinne now. "I'm glad you had people to turn to," she said lightly.

"Me, too."

His harsh profile eased, along with something inside Rina. Something warm, compelling, and far more dangerous than pure sexual desire. Which didn't bode well for an emotionless fling. "Want to tell me about this tradition you two shared?" she asked despite her better judgment.

Standing, he walked to the big window overlooking a neighborhood park. She left the now-cold coffee on the desk corner and followed. In silence, she glanced out over his shoulder. Snow covered the ground and trees in true holiday tradition. There'd be a white Christmas this year, Rina thought.

"Joe's as close to a father as I've got," Colin's voice intruded on her thoughts. "And every year since he took me in, we'd go stalking through the woods in search of the perfect tree."

"You didn't shop for one?" she asked. "Because where I grew up, we chose the cheapest tree off the neighborhood supermarket parking lot."

His deep chuckle warmed her. "No, we played mountain man. We'd go to the far end of Joe's property, which included forest, and we'd pick and cut our own tree." He shoved his hands into his back pockets, staring, she assumed, at the pines behind the building. "We never missed a year, either."

"Until this one," she guessed.

She heard his unspoken words and felt the empty space in his heart as if it were her own. He was still the little boy who'd lost his parents and only had Joe to turn to.

Unable to stop herself, she lifted her hand, letting her palm rest on his shoulder in a gesture of comfort. Heat sizzled on contact, traveling faster than an electric current through her veins, creating a heaviness in her breasts and a slow simmer low in her belly. She should have been prepared.

Instead, she struggled for an even breath. "Corinne says Joe's prognosis *is* good," she said, fighting even harder to concentrate on simple conversation.

He touched her hand briefly, acknowledging her compassion. "It is. But it's hard having him out of commission. A lot of things are tough these days."

His voice was as rough as his skin, both conjuring images of hot nights as his hands skimmed her bare flesh and he muttered raw, sexy words in her ear. She trembled at the carnal, erotic thoughts. Not unexpected for a woman who'd decided she wanted a sexual encounter with the man standing before her. But strange thoughts for a woman who'd liked sex yet had never before *wanted* it this badly.

And she needed him to know she understood his emotions, too. "It's not the same thing, but I know what it's like to miss someone you care about. My brother lives back in New York."

"How many siblings do you have?"

"Just Jake, and believe me, having a cop for an older brother makes up for any other watchful eyes. You try making out on the doorstep after a date while your older brother plays unwanted bodyguard."

Colin laughed and she was grateful to hear the sexy

sound. "Something tells me you've been a handful for him."

His teasing words, along with the rebirth of his light, flirting tone, reminded her she was on a mission. A professional mission to test Colin's awareness of any changes and a personal one to tempt him into being the man with whom she'd begin her affair.

In favor of getting to know Colin and easing his obvious pain she'd almost forgotten her agenda, and as a result, she'd grown closer to him. Emotionally closer, something that hadn't been part of the plan.

But now that he seemed back to his teasing self, she intended to control her feelings better, too. "I've given Jake a run for his money a time or two," she said, keeping things light.

"I just bet you have." He turned her way at last.

She let out a flirtatious laugh before pursing her heavily glossed lips. Like a magnet, his gaze zeroed in on its target and the temperature in the room soared upward. Mission accomplished, she thought. He'd noticed her, though she wasn't certain exactly what had drawn his attention.

Continuing simple conversation wasn't easy with the awareness simmering between them, but she managed. "There was the time I took a vacation," she mused, pretending to concentrate solely on her story. "Then I left him to apartment-sit and neglected to mention I'd invited someone else to join him."

Remembering how Jake and Brianne had gotten together sent shivers of happiness through her. They were proof that two different people could join on an equal footing. Jake allowed Brianne the freedom to be herself while Brianne put up with her brother's macho demeanor without giving up any of her independence in the process.

"Good thing he's a cop. At least he's trained to keep a step or two ahead of you." Lightness shimmered in his expression in complete opposition to his earlier black mood.

If she'd brought him out of his funk, she was glad.

"Jake's got an edge over us poor civilians who you manage to take off guard," he continued.

"I'm easy enough to read."

His gaze roamed over her, settling again on her face. "Oh, no, you're not. Something's different." He studied her, deliberately taking his time and playing her game, a grin on his face. "Same glasses, same type of large, comfortable sweater." He shook his head and Rina held her breath.

She wanted details. What did he notice? What did he like best about the subtle changes? Dammit. She shouldn't care so much. At the very least, she should view him as another means to document results for her column. But unlike the guy at the coffee shop, she did care what Colin thought.

And her body tingled with anticipation and hope that he'd like what he saw. "Come on. You're a reporter. I'm sure observing is your specialty. So, what do you see?"

He raised an eyebrow, then lifted his finger to her cheek, his touch gentle as he glided over her skin. He turned his hand toward her to reveal the combination of foundation and blush that had transferred onto his skin. "What I see is that you look pretty, Rina. Then again, you always do."

The compliment, one that encompassed yesterday's Rina, too, sent nervous flutters to her stomach and a ridiculously pleased rush to her heart.

"But you don't need makeup to enhance what's already beautiful." Male appreciation flickered in his gaze as he leaned forward, those delicious lips a kiss away. "But I have to know. Was the change for me?" he asked.

"You wish," she teased. "I'm experimenting for my column. Just call yourself one man with brilliant powers of observation, that's all." She hoped she sounded nonchalant, though she felt anything but. She *had* thought of him when applying the light shades of color and fixing her hair. Rina swallowed hard. "I already know the guy in the coffee shop downstairs reacted. I just wanted to see if the rest of your species gets as high a grade."

He raised one eyebrow. "You're going to make me compete for your attention?"

"Any reason why I shouldn't?" she asked, deliberately playful. The ability to flirt had returned, Rina thought. And she was enjoying it very much.

"Because I'm not a man who shares easily." His deep gaze told her he was serious.

And now her insides were quaking. He didn't care whether or not she altered her appearance with makeup. He was attracted to her anyway and considering he'd always stared hard and seemed interested, she knew he wasn't lying. But he was screwing up her results for her column and wreaking havoc with her body and her brain.

"Come with me to Emma's Christmas bash Saturday night," he said, changing the subject.

His words surprised her. "As colleagues or something more?" She wanted the rules spelled out, no misunderstandings allowed.

"Call it what you want," he said in a determined voice. "I'll pick you up at eight."

She wanted to go with him, but something about the way he'd ordered her around didn't sit well with her. "If I show up with you, I can't mingle with other men, and the opportunity to research is lost." She treated him to a pout for effect.

"That's the point." Biting back a grin, he folded his arms over his chest. "I want you to myself. Besides, you said yourself you're alone for the holidays."

Actually, she'd only said her brother lived in New York. He was coming to visit next weekend for Christmas Eve, but that didn't seem relevant right now.

"With Joe in the hospital, I'm solo, too. Are you going to make me spend the holidays alone?" Colin's eyes twinkled as he obviously played his trump card.

He knew it, so did she. How could she turn down a man she'd seen in real pain over his father's stroke and the changes Corinne had brought to the office?

"Come on, Rina," he said, resorting to shameless pleading. "Emma's grandson was my college roommate. I know from personal experience the Montgomery family bash is enough to brighten anyone's holiday. It's an event you have to see for yourself. But not alone," he quickly added before she could jump in with that very suggestion.

She eyed him warily.

"If I promise to leave you alone long enough to work your wiles on the unsuspecting men there, will you let me pick you up at eight?" he asked, *giving her a choice.*

She expelled a breath of air. Until that moment, she hadn't realized she'd really been about to say no.

Because his pushing, no matter how flirtatious, made her feel cornered when she wanted to make her own decisions. His insistence, she acknowledged now, had reminded her of Robert, of the times he'd wanted to go to a legal benefit of some sort, and she'd preferred to stay home. Back then, there had never been a compromise. Her husband's way had always prevailed.

The realization surprised her, and she rubbed her hands over her arms, shocked that Colin had provided a parallel to her marriage. An unflattering one at that. But Colin had offered her a real choice now. He honestly cared about her feelings.

Which allowed her to say yes. Pleased and suddenly excited, she met his patient stare, letting her smile grow before she spoke. "Okay. Eight's fine."

His eyes widened. Apparently, she'd surprised him. "I'm glad," he said.

"You'd better be prompt." The night would give her even more opportunity to implement changes and ply her charms on the upper crust of Ashford society. As well as on Colin, she thought with yearning and anticipation.

He grinned. "I wouldn't miss one second of our time together."

Neither would she, and she wondered what other surprises the holidays had in store. "I need to get back to work."

He inclined his head toward her desk. "I'm not stopping you."

Yes, he was. Just by being in the room. She started for her work area, ignoring the curious stares and the feel of Colin's gaze branding her back. For the first time, she realized they'd created a world apart in the crowded office. Talking as if no one else in the room existed. She trembled at the discovery. If he had the power to entrance her so thoroughly in public, she wondered what he'd do if he got her alone. She had this weekend to tease herself with all the exciting possibilities.

And she had Emma's party at which to find out. Because if she had her way, she and Colin I-don't-stick-around Lyons were about to embark on a brief but oh-so-very-satisfying affair.

Chapter Three

S O, RINA CLAIMED the makeup was part of her experiment for her column? Like hell, Colin thought. He'd prefer to think it had something to do with him.

It was no secret he'd been attracted to her from day one, but he hadn't known anything about her. In one brief talk, he'd learned plenty. She'd shocked him by being so down-to-earth and understanding, so interested in his life and his past. He'd turned, intending to thank her. Instead, he'd been surprised by her new look. Rina didn't need makeup to turn him on. But he couldn't deny that her newly made-up face, glowing skin, and full, pink, made-to-be-kissed lips had entranced him anyway. And he wanted to taste that glossy pout again now.

Ever since he'd let down his guard for that kiss, he'd been in a constant state of arousal. And from the minute he'd seen her today, long strands of hair hanging down her back, he'd wanted her even more. Unbelievable but true. He swallowed a groan, feeling as though he'd been sucker-punched because it didn't end there. When she'd let down *her* guard enough to listen to his problems, lust had turned to something a little more. She'd crept under his skin.

She was the first woman who'd affected him on a gut level. Even now, back at their desks, his horizontally next to hers, they sat in aware silence. Every so often, she'd glance his way, her eyes opened wider than usual. And even through the eyeglass lenses, their golden sparkle twinkled at him, extending an invitation, one he wondered whether she was even aware of issuing.

Though he should have invited her to Emma's party as a means to feel her out on the subject of Corinne, his initial reasoning had been far different. He'd be damned if he'd let her spend the holidays alone in a new town, no family, few friends. Not after she'd been there for him at the awful moment he'd been forced to acknowledge Corinne's expensively decorated tree.

When was the last time he'd trusted a woman with his feelings? Certainly, his ex-wife, Julie, had taught him the pain inherent in sharing and the benefit of accounting to no one. After his parents died, travel had always beckoned to him. It didn't take a shrink to figure out that he was running from the pain, but there wasn't a damn thing he could do about his overwhelming desire to go.

As he matured, he'd realized that he could do

some good by combining travel with his journalistic talent and bring world news back home. When Julie had cheated on him, leaving him emotionally as well as physically just as his parents had, it was time to move on. Colin had quit his day job and left the country.

He'd never gotten close to another woman since, yet here he was, sharing his pain with Rina, a woman he barely knew. Ironically, he felt as if she understood him better than Julie ever had. But he had a paper to save, and he couldn't forget his mission again. Couldn't let his goal drop in favor of enjoying Rina's warm, giving personality or sexy new look. If the time seemed right to question her about Corinne, he'd damn well better do it since he had a phone message on his answering machine from the CEO of Fortune's Inc. asking about progress. In reality, the clock was ticking down.

And psychologically, the situation settled on Colin's shoulders in a different way. Both Ron Gold, the lender, and Bert Hartmann, head of Fortune's, their biggest advertiser, were old friends of Joe's and had helped him fund the paper back in its early days. Hartmann currently brought in a huge chunk of change for the paper every year, and the *Times* couldn't afford to lose the company's support. Nor did Colin want to disappoint Joe and have him come back to a sunken ship and lost respect in the eyes of his colleagues. Colin was determined. If nothing else, the *Times* would be on the road to recovery by the time Joe left the hospital.

"'Tis the season to be jolly, fa-la-la-la-la, la-la, la-la." A distinctive, high-pitched voice traveled into the room, and Colin cringed as Corinne, decked out in a designer coat that he knew hadn't come cheap, sauntered through the place.

She swirled through, dispensing tinsel in her wake, and he picked a gold strand off his black sweater.

"I've come to invite you all to a Christmas party," she said.

Her voice grated on his nerves. So did her words. "Emma's family is having a party Saturday night." His objective was to bail out the paper. He didn't need her spending any more cash they didn't have. "We're all invited, so why don't you save money and celebrate there?"

"Oh, don't be a spoilsport, Colin," Rina said. "It's nice of Corinne to want to show her employees holiday spirit and a good time."

Which cemented for him whose side Rina was on. Of course, he doubted Corinne had informed her of the paper's precarious financial position. He couldn't fault Rina for having holiday spirit and let her comment slide. But after their talk today, Colin understood Rina a little better, too. She hadn't grown up wealthy.

That put him in a better position to appeal to her regarding Corinne's excessive spending—once he felt more sure she'd trust where his interests lay.

"Rina's right." Corinne smiled and readjusted the collar of her coat. "I'm glad to see someone here appreciates me."

"Don't kid yourself, Corinne. I appreciate you and everything you stand for," Colin muttered.

Rina coughed and he glanced over. Her eyebrows were raised but she said nothing.

Intelligent and circumspect, she'd obviously picked up the undercurrents and decided to let things play out without interrupting.

"Everyone, listen." Corinne clapped her hands and all heads lifted from computer screens, keyboards, and layouts in order to glance up. "We're having a party Friday night at the Seaside Restaurant. Guests welcome." With another toss of tinsel, she started for the door.

"Corinne, wait," Colin called.

She turned.

"Where are you going?" he asked mildly.

"To plan the menu." She hiked her bag back onto her shoulder. "I also want to buy token appreciation gifts for the staff. Joe would want that." She sniffed and lifted a hand as if to blot a tear from her eye.

Colin couldn't tell if the sentiment was real or

phony. With Corinne, he didn't know her well enough to be sure. "You'd do Joe more good by staying at the hospital instead. Be with your husband." Corinne was supposed to take the morning shift while Colin covered afternoons. "And while you're at it, ask Joe if he'd want you spending what's left of the budget on a party," he said so only she could hear.

She waved a hand, dismissing his concerns. "I refuse to bother Joe when he needs his strength to recover. Besides, you worry too much."

"And you don't worry enough. Bert Hartmann called, reminding us of Fortune's Inc.'s deadline. You need to get Joe to transfer power of attorney back to me or sign a good-faith promise to change the paper's direction." He ran a frustrated hand through his hair. "Hell, Corinne, just start running legitimate news. That'll get us through the new year without losing our biggest advertiser." He heard the pleading in his voice and didn't care.

She shook her head. "It'd be based on false pretenses, Colin, because I believe in my vision." Corinne turned away, effectively ending the conversation.

Which was just as well. If she continued, he might throttle her. He didn't need to wonder why he rarely came home when the frustrating reason stood in front of him.

"Emma," Corinne called as she started for the

door. "Colin seems a little stressed. Maybe you could work on fixing *him* up next."

He rolled his eyes.

Emma laughed, rubbing her hands together in a sure sign of trouble.

And Rina pursed those luscious lips in blatant disapproval at Corinne's suggestion. Just the sight of her eased the tension in his neck and shoulders, making him think of more pleasurable things. Like her warm body in his bed, writhing against his cool sheets.

"I'm sure Colin can choose his own women," Rina said, more possessively than he'd expected.

He grinned. "What's the matter? Worried Emma will find someone who'll distract me from you?"

She tossed her head. "Not a chance. I'm secure enough in what I have to offer."

He met her gaze, holding on and not letting go. "That's good to know. But even if you weren't, you have nothing to worry about. Once I set my sights on a goal, I'm totally focused."

And his goal was now twofold. On the one hand, he had to live up to the standards Joe had set and to make sure he even had a paper left when he recovered. And in doing so, he'd prove to himself that he hadn't let the old man down.

But where Rina was concerned, he couldn't discount the attraction. He wanted more from her than to be colleagues who'd kissed once.

How much more remained to be seen.

ONCE I SET my sights on a goal, I'm totally focused. Days later, Rina couldn't shake Colin's words from her mind because his steely gaze told her he *was* focused—and *she* was his objective. She shivered, unsure if it was chemistry and excitement fluttering inside her or pure nerves because tonight was Emma's infamous party and Colin was her date.

She'd had the whole week to anticipate this one night. Friday evening she'd gone to Corinne's party expecting to see Colin. Instead, he'd been a no-show. Considering his negative attitude toward Joe's wife, she didn't have to wonder why he'd skipped the event. Apparently, if something made Colin uncomfortable, he opted out. Out of the event, and sometimes out of the country. She couldn't afford to miss him too much.

At the office holiday party, most of the men at work were married or otherwise taken, so Rina had socialized with the women. She'd used the night wisely, taking notes on their views of what men wanted and what would attract and keep the opposite sex interested. Most women agreed that while men were attracted to packaging, only something deeper and far beyond chemistry would keep one around.

But packaging most always jump-started a relationship, and her first column in her *Simply Sexy* series, entitled "Sex Appeal," had run on Thursday. If the e-mails and phone calls were any indication, she'd made a huge impact on the reading audience already.

As she'd emailed the link to the column to Jake and Brianne, pride had swelled inside her. So had new and revealing feelings. This job filled an emptiness within her, and she owed Corinne a huge debt for giving her this chance.

Next week's article was called "Strut Your Stuff." The title was courtesy of Emma, the idea something Rina had learned how to do during her years in New York. She'd been a single woman in Manhattan, and her married life had consisted of parties, social get-togethers, and business dinners. Her past provided her with a solid knowledge base. She knew how to act in order to attract a man as she'd proven with the coffee shop owner the other day. Her conversations with women both in the past and the present provided added insight.

Once she'd been able to put Colin out of her mind, she'd gotten a good, strong start on her series. But Colin never left her thoughts for long. They'd connected on a deeper level, proving that the dance they'd begun could be more than just hot. An affair with

Colin could be dangerous if she didn't keep her emotions under lock and key.

✧   ✧   ✧

A SMART MAN knew when to give a woman space. Colin prided himself on possessing enough intelligence to stay the hell away from Rina until Saturday, letting the anticipation build. Besides, he didn't want to give her the opportunity to break their date and ruin any chance he'd have to learn more about her.

She rented a small upstairs apartment in a Cape-style house. He knew this because Emma had handed him Rina's address along with directions. "In case you get lost. Wouldn't want you driving in circles all night when you could be with Rina," the older woman had said, winking. Clearly she knew nothing about navigation systems in cars and on cell phones.

At eight sharp, he rang Rina's doorbell. The last thing he expected was to be greeted by a barking dog. From behind the door, he heard Rina's command. "Norton, sit."

Norton? What kind of name was Norton?

She opened the door, but before he could catch a glimpse of Rina, he was attacked by the dog, who jumped up on his hind legs and placed his front paws on Colin's lower thighs.

"Norton, down!" Rina grabbed the dog's collar

and jerked him off.

Norton complied with a sad whine.

"I'm sorry," she said. "His manners are usually better than that."

Colin laughed. "At least he has some manners." He glanced down at Norton, seeing him for the first time. "A shar-pei?"

She pet the dog's tan head, then meshed her fingers through the wrinkles on his back. "What was your first clue?" she asked wryly.

He'd never seen the breed anywhere except television and knew nothing about them except they cost a pretty penny. He'd never pictured Rina with this kind of breed, but he liked the dog immediately. "He's a gorgeous animal."

She smiled. "He was Robert's dog before I ever came along. Now he's mine."

At the mention of a male name, one said with a sadness tinged with regret, Colin's stomach twisted. He couldn't remember the last time any woman had evoked jealousy inside him, not even Julie. Rina was different, as his churning insides reminded him.

Had she left a man behind in New York? At the thought, the pain in his stomach became acute. "Who's Robert?" he asked, his jaw aching from the tension of gritting his teeth.

"My husband."

His gut clenched violently. "You're—"

"But he died," she added quickly. "I just hate the word *widow*."

That took some of the wind out of him. He started to reach for her, then, unsure the gesture was appropriate, merely said, "I'm sorry."

"Thanks." She patted Norton and rose. "It's been a while now."

As soon as she'd removed her hand from the dog's collar, Norton walked over to Colin and began sniffing at his feet.

"Uh… you should watch out. He peed on my brother's sneakers the first time they met. He's particular about who he likes."

Colin laughed, and the tension broke, but he stepped back just in case. Norton followed, rubbing his head against Colin's pant leg. Following the dog's lead, Colin gave him the attention he desired and scratched the dog's head. In response, Norton flopped into a prone position before rolling onto his back, legs spread open wide.

"Ugh. Norton, have some class," Rina groaned. "He likes to expose himself. It's embarrassing."

She met his gaze, amusement and something more bubbling in the brown depths that he just now noticed weren't covered by the black-framed glasses. He stepped back to admire the change. Her face had the same minimal makeup as he'd noticed the day before, but without the glasses, he got an unobstructed view of those gorgeous eyes—and he liked what he saw.

"I hope you don't mind, but I need to walk Norton before we go. I'll dress for the party as soon as we get back." She turned toward the coatrack and the ponytail swung behind her, hitting the center of her back. "My landlord's washing machine broke while I was doing laundry and I spent the afternoon at the laundromat," she explained. "I never had time to change." Reaching for her jacket, she shrugged it on over her shoulders, then grabbed Norton's leash.

"I'll go with you to walk the pooch," he offered.

Sixty minutes later, they finally returned home with Norton in tow. Colin's fingertips were frozen and his nose was numb. "You did this on purpose, didn't you?" he asked.

"Did what?"

Her wide questioning gaze might have fooled other men but not one with a reporter's instincts. "You waited for me to walk Norton, knowing it was an hour ordeal so I could freeze to death along with you," he said wryly.

Not that he'd minded their time walking, talking and just getting to know one another even more. If anything, she'd defeated her purpose. He felt closer to her now than ever before. The one thing he hadn't been able to bring up was the subject of Corinne and the paper since Rina had dominated the conversation with stories of her childhood Christmases. Even with little money, they'd always had warm, family times.

Something Joe and Nell had tried to give to him. Looking back, he hadn't made it easy, going so far as to stay at friends' homes to avoid the stark reality of his parents' absence. Listening to Rina, her easy chatter and comfortable silences, allowed him to reflect, to acknowledge his actions and regret them. But it was Joe who needed to know his feelings, and while he was home this time, Colin intended to make amends.

"I just wanted you to share the fun Norton brings to my life." She met his gaze, amusement and happiness in those brown depths.

She made him feel good. "You mean his unique quirks. He hates the ice-cold street so much that he tries to dive for shelter into any home we pass. Doing business is the last thing on his mind."

"He might have a slight problem with weather extremes," she admitted.

"Which prolongs his walk."

She bit the inside of her lip. "I didn't say that."

He let out a feigned groan. "You didn't have to. I figure you wanted my company on Norton's long walk."

"My brother always says I'm chronically late, so

you really can't think I stalled walking him on purpose." Her lips twitched, a sure sign she'd been caught.

The desire to kiss those lips grew stronger inside him. He wanted to linger here and to hell with Emma's holiday bash. "Any chance you'd go change so we can get going?"

Because if she didn't, he'd act on his impulses, carrying her to the couch across from the TV and kissing her again. Only this time, he wouldn't stop with her lips. He'd feast on her skin as well and hoped she'd do the same on his.

"I'll be ready in five minutes." Her voice brought him out of his fantasy.

"I've never known a woman yet who could be ready that fast, especially one with a chronic lateness problem."

She laughed. "Just watch me." Catching her turn of phrase, she blushed. "I didn't mean literally watch me. I meant just wait for me. And see." She started for the open door on the other side of the room. "Norton will keep you company." Then she slipped inside and slammed the door shut behind her.

He refused to let his mind wander to thoughts of her undressing in the next room. He couldn't if he wanted to be able to walk into Emma's party. Instead, he shot a sideways glance at the pooch who sat at his feet, black tongue hanging out as he panted from the exertion of his walk. "I'm sure there's water for you somewhere." Colin headed for the kitchen, a small room off the living area.

Norton followed, and sure enough, his bowl sat in a corner and he ran for it, devouring the water in thirsty laps. With the dog occupied, Colin went back to the family room for a better look into who Rina Lowell really was.

In a bookcase, he found mystery novels, which didn't surprise him since the woman appeared to be an enigma herself. He also discovered a framed photo of a dark-haired man and a woman with her arms around his neck. Since the man had similar features to Rina, he assumed the guy was her brother, Jake, and the woman his wife, Brianne. An older couple with palm trees in the background waved for the camera. Her parents, he assumed. And finally, another of Rina, hair pulled back as usual, her arms around Norton. Colin grinned, liking the mix of family photos. His own rented condo held similar ones. An old shot of his parents and more recent ones of Joe and Nell. It seemed both he and Rina had a soft spot for family.

Already and without trying he'd discovered common ground. The explosive, hot chemistry they already shared went without saying. Their caring for family was a strong indication that they shared other needs as well. Needs he'd be only too happy to cultivate while satiating their mutual desires at the same time.

It didn't escape his notice that he hadn't seen a picture of her late husband, and his curiosity grew. The corner of the room had a small wooden desk. A small photo sat on the corner and he found himself drawn there. And because the picture was a small, framed, wallet-size one and set apart from the photos in plain view, a twinge of guilt nudged at him, but he picked up the picture anyway.

A too-good-looking guy stared back at him. Colin hadn't known Rina long, but he didn't see her with the suit-and-tie, corporate type. Then again, he wouldn't have envisioned her with a shar-pei, either, and the dog was back, slobbering at his feet. Proof that where Rina was concerned, he should expect the unexpected. He liked the intrigue and challenge she presented.

Why not? He was a man who thrived on extremes. Rina, who lacked artifice and possessed extraordinary depth, offered him many layers to uncover and revel in.

He replaced the picture and stepped back to the center of the room just as Rina reentered. He took one look at her and his libido, which he'd been barely controlling, kicked into high gear. How it this woman managed to look sexy in a tuxedo?

Colin wore black pants and a sport jacket with a

mock turtleneck sweater beneath, the most he'd do in the way of dress-up. Rina had her own mode of dress. His gaze traveled from her black pumps, up her tailored slacks, to the white-collared shirt with suspenders and red bow tie. His exploration didn't end there but continued to her face, adorned only by the sheer foundation and blush, her wide eyes, which had some shadow and mascara, and settled on her red lips. She wasn't in a sexy dress nor did she display ample cleavage, yet she simply took his breath away.

Was it his imagination or had the oxygen been sucked out of the room? He drew a shallow breath.

"I'm ready to go." She glanced at her watch. "With thirty seconds to spare."

"And a damn fine job you did in those five minutes." He extended his hand, and she came toward him.

"Well, thank you. Did I mention you dress up nicely yourself?"

He grasped her elbow, then without warning he realized what else was different about her tonight. "Your hair."

"It's still here, right? I haven't gone bald since I left you earlier?" She lifted a hand to the shoulder-length strands and laughed.

"No, but it's a damn sight shorter than the ponytail led me to believe."

"The art of illusion, Colin. Women are masters. I take it you liked my extension?"

Enough to give him a damn hard-on as he'd day-dreamed about wrapping himself in the silken mass. "I liked it," he said blandly.

She leaned closer and a hint of peppermint drifted toward him. He wasn't sure if it came from her toothpaste or her shampoo, but she smelled fresh, clean, and distractingly sexy. No expensive perfumed scents for Rina. And Colin found himself even more aroused by her natural scent.

"Liar," she said softly in his ear. "You *loved* the po-nytail. Because men love long hair. It's the stuff of fantasies."

"Says who?" He folded his arms across his chest in a deliberate attempt to play dumb. He might act like a stereotypical male but damned if he'd admit to it. Besides, the feelings she aroused in him weren't contingent on what she wore or how she looked.

"Every woman's magazine printed."

"Oh, yeah? Then why does this shaggy hairdo turn me on?" He went for the personal question instead of pursuing his professional agenda. Rather than jump on the opportunity to ask if she'd ever considered taking her talents to a more appropriate venue like one of those magazines she'd mentioned, he opted to let her know what she did to him. He turned her way, captur-ing her between his body and the wall, not allowing her room to maneuver away.

She sucked in a breath and her nipples tightened, pressing into his chest. He wanted desperately to run his fingers through her tousled hair but refrained, knowing they were ready to leave and he'd cause yet another delay if he did. "You could test a saint," he said with a low groan.

"I'm not trying to test a saint," she said in a teasing voice. "I'm trying to test you."

"And you're doing a damn good job." But this physical thing between them had to wait. "Time to party." He held out his hand.

Confusion settled in her eyes.

"Didn't you say you wanted to use Emma's family party to research?"

She nodded. "I did."

"Well, I don't want you to resent me because you didn't get your job done." He didn't want to give her an excuse to push him away—and not just because Joe's legacy was at stake. He wanted Rina to believe what she wanted and needed was important to him. Because suddenly, it was.

She tipped her head to the side. "Are you for real?"

"Last time I looked." Though he admitted to himself that he was sure off balance now. He had a job to do and he couldn't afford to care for Rina or her needs.

Unfortunately, he already did.

Chapter Four

AFTER THE HEATED sexual tension in her apartment and later in the car, Rina welcomed the relief brought by the cold winter air. Snow flurries fell around them, making it feel like Christmas. With Colin at her side, his hand beneath her elbow, she walked into the Montgomerys' incredibly beautiful Tudor-style home.

She'd looked forward to the huge party both Emma and Colin had described, but when she stepped into the marble entryway, instead of joyous holiday spirit, an uneasy sense of déjà vu enveloped her instead. The Montgomery mansion reminded her of the New York City penthouse she'd shared with her husband. The place her brother, Jake, called the mausoleum because of the marble floors and the crystal and china decor. She'd always known the apartment wasn't her style but seeing this mansion with distance from her past life cemented the notion. She much preferred the homey upstairs apartment she rented. But she had Colin by her side to take away the past, and she intended to enjoy the here and now.

"Coatroom's this way," Colin said, oblivious to her

inner turmoil.

And Rina intended to keep it that way. She accompanied him to where a woman dressed as one of Santa's elves sat taking coats and handing out numbers, and she checked her wool coat.

"Isn't this place something?" he asked.

She hoped he wasn't as impressed as he sounded. "Beautiful, but too… everything," she said, unwilling to put her feelings into words.

"Yeah. I couldn't see myself growing up in a place like this." He glanced around and shuddered. "Too many damn things to break."

She laughed, relieved he wasn't comfortable, either. "Why can I see you throwing a ball in the house and getting grounded?"

He leaned over and whispered in her ear. "Because I'm a bad boy?"

His voice was deep, his breath warm, and a rush of air trickled over her skin and her stomach fluttered, settling low with damp heat.

"I like bad boys," she murmured, and his gaze dilated with desire. Then, because they were in public, she stepped back and looked around her. "This isn't a place to raise kids, that's for sure."

"Kids, huh?"

As soon as the words escaped, she'd wanted to snatch them back, the notion too intimate to discuss with the man who made her libido jump. Who had her thinking illicit thoughts, like what it would feel like to run her hands through his windblown hair and warm her chilled body by cuddling naked with him. And when those blue eyes stared into hers, she had a hunch he saw the feelings and heard the thoughts she'd imagined but hadn't spoken aloud.

She shrugged, trying to keep things light. "What can I say? This place doesn't exactly inspire the image of hearth and home."

Rina wasn't sure if she'd ever remarry let alone have children, and considering her current fear of emotional involvement, the prospect seemed unlikely. But Jake and Brianne planned for kids and Rina wanted to be an aunt who had sleepovers and provided fun and a safe haven, not a place where they had to tiptoe and be quiet for fear of breaking something.

She glanced around once more, taking in the Christmas decorations. An exquisite tree sat in the corner and red satin bows covered the circular staircase. Her New York apartment had once been wrapped in similar red satin, she thought, remembering. A professional Robert had hired chose the holiday decorations for the penthouse. To make her life easier, he'd said. In order to impress friends and clients, she'd thought. And Rina had missed the down-to-earth Christmases she'd shared with her family.

"Take a look," Colin said, pointing to the elves in green serving hors d'oeuvres.

Rina laughed, her mood lightening. "The party theme seems more down-to-earth than the decor or the furnishings, if that makes any sense."

"That's because the caterer is as down-to-earth as you can get. Emma's granddaughter-in-law owns a company called Pot Luck. That's how they met, and she's been doing the parties here ever since. They've been together ever since, too."

"Sounds as if you like her," Rina said.

He nodded. "I do. Cat's special."

"I see." She didn't like hearing him gush about another woman's charms, not one bit. Not even if said woman was married to his friend.

"Do you? Actually, Catherine Montgomery is very much like you." A smile twitched at his lips, but before he could say more, Emma padded up to them in her gown and ballet-type slippers at a near run. Considering the gleaming marble floors, Emma possessed amazing agility for a woman her age.

"There you are! And not a minute too soon. I need you to hide me," Emma said.

"Excuse me?" Rina couldn't have heard right.

"Hide me. I'm being followed by a lecher."

Colin rolled his eyes and laughed.

"Gran, you get back here," a male voice called as a

good-looking man with dark hair joined their growing group.

"Hey, Logan," Colin said.

"Logan, Emma's grandson?" Rina asked. Though now that she studied him, she recognized him from the photos on Emma's desk.

"The one and only. Who's this pretty lady?" he asked Colin, but his gaze remained locked on Rina.

Heat rushed to her cheeks at his compliment and her newly acquired professional instincts rushed into high gear. Logan Montgomery had manners and a wedding ring on his hand. Still, Rina couldn't discount the approval in his gaze when he studied her. She'd seen the same admiration in the eyes of the parking attendant when he'd helped her out of Colin's car. Attitude plus appearance equaled attention, Rina thought and made a mental note to mention the dual impact in her next column.

Before her manners deserted her, she turned back to the people surrounding her. "I'm Rina Lowell."

"I've heard so much about you." Logan took her hand. "Gran adores you and I can see why."

"Why, thank you, Mr. Montgomery." She fluttered her lashes at Logan and graced him with a smile.

"You're quite welcome."

"And you're quite married," Colin muttered and not-so-discreetly slid his grasp to her hand, disengaging Logan's grip and marking his territory.

She tried to tug her hand free, but he held on fast. "I didn't know you were the jealous type," she said under her breath, suddenly enjoying his possessiveness.

"I didn't know that about him, either," Logan laughed.

And though Rina recognized good-natured ribbing between friends, she had the unexpected urge to protect Colin from any jokes directed his way. "I've heard so much about you from Emma, too. Where's Catherine? I've been looking forward to meeting her."

"Her company, Pot Luck, is catering this party." Pride filled his voice, and it was obvious no woman could compete for Logan Montgomery's affection except his wife. "She's going crazy keeping things running smoothly, but as soon as she comes out of the kitchen, I'll bring her by."

"Please do." It was a lucky woman who had not just her husband's love but his approval to do or be anything she wanted. Catherine had both, and even without knowing the other woman, Rina was glad.

"As for you, Gran..." Logan turned to his grandmother.

"I'd hoped you'd forgotten all about me," Emma said, a wistful note in her voice.

"Stan Blecher wants to take you to the Boston

Pops and you can't keep running off and ignoring the man. He's a federal court judge, and much as I don't get swayed by status, you can't be rude. You'll dig a hole for the judge and for yourself," he said pointedly.

Rina sensed the friction and undercurrents between grandmother and grandson but wasn't sure of the cause. As if sensing her unasked question, Colin leaned in closer. "Emma has problems with her son. They call him the judge. Logan asked me to get Emma a job with the paper so the judge wouldn't put her in a retirement home," he whispered.

"*You* got Emma a job?" Rina asked, surprised by the news.

"He did it as a favor. Because my son's a stuffed shirt." Emma sniffed, her regal nose in the air, yet her caring tone proved she loved her only child anyway. "But his colleague's a lecher."

Logan shook his head. "Not accurate, Gran. His last name's Blecher, and you're just being rude. Now, come back inside before Dad gets wind of this."

"Oh, all right. But I'm going to redirect his attention, of that you can be sure." Emma placed her weathered hand on Rina's cheek. "I'm so glad you're here. We'll talk later." She sashayed away with grace, her dress trailing on the floor behind her.

"I should go watch out for her," Logan muttered. "I'll find Cat and we'll meet up again soon," he promised Rina, then disappeared into the crowd.

Rina smiled. "I love Emma and Logan's family dynamics. And as for your connection to them, I didn't know you'd gotten Emma her position at the paper." She met his gaze, knowing it was impossible to hide the respect she'd just gained for him and not caring if he saw.

"Are you saying you didn't know I had a kind streak?" His husky voice reverberated in her ear.

"Not any more than I knew you had a jealous one." She just now realized he still held her hand in his grasp, his thumb tracing erotic circles inside her palm. She shivered, unable to control the impulse.

"I enjoy your sense of humor, Rina. And I enjoy you."

And she enjoyed him. Too much, she thought. Though she'd already chosen him as the man with whom she'd set herself free, she still needed to protect her heart. No matter how charming, the man was a wanderer capable of leaving on a whim.

Already, she knew Colin wouldn't be a man easy to forget. "I need a drink."

"Cat makes a delicious punch. Come on."

After finishing a sherbet-and-champagne-laced drink, Rina relaxed. She held another glass in her hand, and with Colin close by her side, she was enjoying the party. "So, tell me more about getting Emma that job."

"What's to tell?" Colin shrugged. "About a year ago, Logan called and asked me for a favor. Everyone adores Emma, so I talked Joe into hiring her."

"You did more than that. You saved her from her meddling self."

He shrugged, obviously unwilling to admit that he had a caring nature, one that extended beyond Joe, beyond family. With each new fact she learned about Colin, she discovered an intriguing side, making her want to know more.

"I got her a desk job. I didn't know she'd end up writing a singles column, though." His eyebrows furrowed, aggravation plain on his face.

She didn't understand why. "Something wrong with what Emma writes?"

"It's just an unusual slant for a newspaper to take."

She nodded. "I thought so, too, the first time I heard about what Corinne was doing with the *Times*." During their initial conversation, Corinne had explained her vision of using the paper as a means to bring the town together. She believed that in today's world, people needed more warmth and compassion and less harsh reality.

Under her leadership, the *Times* would advertise where people could meet. Men and women would learn how to relate to one another better when they did mingle at a social event. While the paper would still be reporting some news, the focus would be on people. Listening to Corinne's excitement, Rina knew she'd found a place to call home.

Colin folded his arms over his chest. "So how did you come to work for Corinne?"

"Hors d'oeuvre?" An elf stopped by with a tray in hand.

The delicious aroma tickled her nose, but Rina was more interested in her conversation with Colin than with the food on the plate. "No, thank you."

Colin shook his head and the woman in green took her leave.

"You were telling me about how you came to work for Corinne?" he prompted the moment they were alone again.

"Oh, it's a long story. Basically, my parents knew hers. I heard about Corinne taking over her husband's paper, thought my writing would interest her, and I called."

"You pursued your goals," he said with approval. "Did you always want to be a writer?"

She shook her head. "No, I took the long route. I used to be a legal secretary. The hours were decent, the pay was guaranteed, and so was the overtime. It covered the bills, but I'd always been more a people person than someone who liked being holed up in an office."

"That much I can believe." His warm gaze met hers, mesmerizing her so much it was hard to realize they were still at a party surrounded by people.

She tipped her head to one side. "I'm hoping that's a compliment and not a dig at my curious nature."

"I admire you, Rina."

The husky tone in his voice sent shivers of awareness down her spine. "Thanks," she murmured.

"And your writing…"

"I always took notes, wrote stories. Anecdotes." She shrugged, remembering. "After I got married, I had a lot of free time to fill pages in a journal."

At first, she'd used her new surroundings and her husband's new friends as subjects. She'd been amused by the for-show marriages she'd witnessed and enthralled by the real relationships, like her parents', that had lasted for years. Her observations had become humorous slice-of-life stories that kept her busy while home alone.

"You stopped working?" he asked, apparently truly interested in her past.

Why wouldn't he be? She was equally interested in his. "My husband wanted to give me the life he thought I always wanted. But staying home and spending money I hadn't earned, well, that just wasn't me."

But to please Robert, she'd eventually accepted the lifestyle. After all, most women would have traded anything to be in her position, or so she'd been told at the going-away party the other secretaries had thrown on her last day of work.

"I can't see you staying at home and eating bon-bons, either."

"What can you see me doing?" She wondered how he viewed her.

He shrugged. "A headstrong, determined woman like you? I can see you dissecting what men want." His lips twitched in a wry grin. "The question is whether you'll get it right."

"You're just worried I'll get inside your head."

"You already came close. I read your first article."

"And?" she asked, knowing that right or wrong, his opinion was important to her.

"You made some very valid points. Men *are* visual animals. We see, we react."

"Basic chemistry."

He nodded. "Lust." His voice grew deeper.

"Not enough for anything meaningful or lasting." She cleared her dry throat. "Which is why I have to dig deeper."

"I'm certain you'll dig into both men's and women's psyches." His eyes danced with certainty.

"You think you know me so well?"

He nodded. "I know I do." But he frowned, seemingly not thrilled with the notion.

And Rina thought she knew why. Despite the banter, the notion of getting past lust and digging deeper made him uncomfortable. He wasn't looking for anything more serious than she was. Yet in the short time they'd known one another, he understood her better than Robert ever had. Her husband had loved her and given her everything—except the freedom to be herself. The more time she spent in Ashford, the more time she spent with Colin, the more self-awareness she gained and the more she felt she had to contribute to her work. Not to mention she was coming to enjoy herself. A lot.

"Tell me something. Doesn't it strike you as odd that a newspaper has two relationship columnists?" he asked. "I mean, why write what you do for a paper?"

She really didn't understand what he was getting at. "As opposed to what?"

He shrugged. "An online blog? A magazine, print or online, maybe? There are plenty of those in Manhattan."

"I needed to get away from the memories. To start over fresh. Plus, I had no connections with the publishers there. Corinne was willing to give me a chance. And I liked her vision. She wants to bring people together and is using the newspaper to do it. My writing fits in well here."

He exhaled hard. "But you don't think her *vision*—the subjects she wants to focus on—is odd for a news*paper*?"

"Slightly unusual, maybe. But then, so is the world lately. Besides, many papers, online or print, have articles and columns in the lifestyle section geared toward relationships or other things."

"True. But those papers have an abundance of sections and space. The *Times* is small paper. Space is limited. By adding more frivolous things to it, other sections have to go."

Rina bit her lip and nodded. "I suppose. But Corinne said the *Globe* outsells the *Times* anyway," she said, speaking of the larger competition. "Which freed her up to try something different. All I know is, I owe Corinne for giving me a new start and a new life. And you can't imagine how badly I needed that new life."

He glanced out into the crowd for a moment. "Rina…"

She followed his gaze and realized Emma was barreling through the crowd toward them, an older gentleman hot on her heels. "I wonder what she's up to."

Rina barely got the words out when Emma reached their side, tripped, and knocked her full champagne flute forward. In shock, Rina put up her hand to ward off a spill and ended up tipping the glass onto Colin, too, so they were both covered in champagne.

Rina pulled at the damp shirt, lifting it off her skin. But the damage had been done, and when she released the fabric again, her sheer, lacy bra showed through. The one Rina wore for herself and not for her column and experiment. The one not meant to be seen by the public at large.

Rina didn't know who took notice because she was too caught up in Colin's openmouthed stare as he took in her now-damp, see-through blouse. As if they were alone and not in a room full of people, her nipples puckered in pure female reaction.

"Oh, my, I'm sorry." Emma began fluttering around Rina, ignoring the man by her side who had to be none other than Stan Blecher.

Rina lifted her hands to cover herself. "It's fine, Emma, really."

"No, no, it's not okay. Let me take you up to dry off."

"Emma..." the man said, clearly wishing a moment of her time.

Rina studied the gentleman. He was tall and stood proud, with a full head of white hair and a nice smile. Dentures or real teeth, he cut a dashing figure. "Emma, come on. Give the man a chance," Rina whispered in her ear.

"Nonsense. Grace left some old clothes in her closet. I'm sure we can find a top for you to wear. And for you, Colin, Logan has a sweater or two I can surely scrounge up. Come, come." She motioned with her hands and turned her back on Stan.

Knowing Emma wouldn't be deterred, Rina shrugged and motioned for Colin to follow.

"I'll be here when you get back," Stan called.

"Lecher," Emma muttered.

"I think he's cute," Rina said on her way up the stairs.

Emma ignored her. Apparently, like Rina, the older woman preferred to be the matchmaker, not on the receiving end.

"Colin, this is Logan and Cat's room when they stay here. Which isn't often, but still... Feel free to go into the closet and find a shirt." She opened a door, pushed Colin inside, and slammed the door shut behind him.

"You're a bulldozer, Emma. And you can't run from Stan forever. What's wrong if you have dinner with the man?" Rina asked.

"I've been on my own too long." Emma paused at the next door in the long hall. "This is a bathroom. Go on in here and I'll bring you a shirt of Gracie's, okay?"

"That's sweet, Emma. I'd appreciate it." Before the

older woman could walk out, Rina felt compelled to add something else. "Remember that alone's lonely." And she wondered if she was speaking for her own benefit as well.

Two minutes later, Emma returned with a white oxford shirt, as close a match as she was likely to get. The older woman excused herself, then said she'd meet up with Rina again downstairs.

Rina locked herself in the bathroom and began unbuttoning the wet blouse, parting the material. She found a guest towel she could dampen and turned on the water to wipe the stickiness off her chest when, without warning, a loud creaking noise startled her. She jerked around toward the sound, which had come from behind, only to discover the door didn't lead to a linen closet as she'd originally thought but to the bedroom next door.

And the person who'd entered wasn't Emma but a shirtless, breathtaking Colin.

BEFORE EMMA HAD doused them with champagne, Colin had been trying to get his mind around the concept of how important this job was to Rina and how he could accomplish *his* goals without hurting her. He'd thought to get close enough to divulge the problems with the paper and see if she could give him insight into bringing Corinne around. But both women seemed to need this direction the paper was taking, and damned if Colin knew what to do about it.

Then fate had interrupted in the form of an aging whirling dervish and all conversation and thought stopped, especially when he'd seen Rina in that see-through blouse. He'd broken into a sweat at the sight of all that lace and skin.

By the time he'd stepped into the bathroom to splash cold water on his chest to wash off the sticky champagne, he thought he had himself under control. He hadn't expected to find Rina there. Now that he had, one look and never mind a splash of water, he needed a full-blown, cold shower.

He'd wondered what she hid beneath her bulky clothes, and though tonight's blouse had given him a hint, he hadn't been prepared for the impact. White lace peeked out from behind a hand towel, and thanks to her bra of choice, small but sensually rounded cleavage pushed upward in a tantalizing, tempting V. He tried to swallow but his throat had grown dry.

"A gentleman would say excuse me, turn around, and walk out," Rina said wryly, not a hint of sincerity in her voice.

Even her attempt at covering herself had grown pathetic. Her hands trembled slightly and the towel revealed more than it hid. Her trousers were low-cut, allowing him a glimpse at her creamy skin, and the waist hit just below her belly button, teasing him with a slight indentation tailor-made for a man's tongue.

His tongue, Colin thought. He stepped into the bathroom, closing the door behind him and pushing the lock shut tight. "I don't remember claiming to be a gentleman. Especially when you're around."

"I need to understand this," she murmured.

He liked her intellectual side, the side that refused to give in to instinct without rationale. "What's so difficult to understand? You're a beautiful woman and I'm attracted to you." He took a step closer, inhaling the scent of champagne, wanting to lick the flavor off her skin.

"And you don't care which Rina you're looking at, the one with makeup or without, the one with the long hair or this *shaggy* look." Her voice caught, a hint of awe in her tone.

"That's right. And it's the woman who's researching your column who's surprised. But the woman in here—" He touched her chest with his calloused finger. "That's who you really are. And you know me—just like I know you. And I wouldn't lie just to…"

"Get laid?" she asked, tongue in cheek. "No, I don't think you'd do such a dirty, despicable, male thing." Her lips twitched and a sparkle lit her gaze.

She laughed, and he was glad she had a sense of humor about something many women would make an issue of. He closed the distance between them. They were alone in the small bathroom, not another guest within hearing distance. If Colin had to guess, even Emma was long gone by now. He was certain she'd somehow set them up or at least allowed them time to take advantage of the proximity she'd provided.

Something he had every intention of doing if the woman beside him was willing. And he intended to find out.

Chapter Five

SHOULD SHE OR shouldn't she? Rina didn't want to think any more than she wanted to hesitate. She'd hoped for this moment, and fate only provided so many opportunities. She wanted Colin, and it had been too long since a man had made her feel so desired, so needed. Gathering her courage, she dropped the towel and backed toward the vanity, grasping onto the Corian countertops with both hands. Her position had the erotic effect of pushing her breasts upward in silent invitation.

His gaze slid down to her chest and he let out a slow groan. "Honey, that's going to have to mean yes."

"Yes" to what, she wasn't certain, and at the moment she didn't care. Arousal settled low and dampened her panties, excitement a companion she barely recognized, it had been so long. "I'm so glad you're a man who knows how to read a woman's signals," she said at the same moment he dipped his head, nestling his face between her breasts.

He exhaled slowly, the warmth of his breath hitting her skin as he began to taste the champagne with luxurious laps of his tongue. Starting in her cleavage, he worked his way outward, teasing her with nibbles and tastes until her nipples tightened into rigid peaks begging for equal treatment. He was tormenting her, taking his time, making a slow feast of her flesh until every nerve tingled and desire so overwhelmed her, she whimpered aloud.

He lifted his head, his blue eyes glittering with banked desire. "Tell me what you want."

"Is that what men like?" she asked. "To be told?"

"I'm not going to answer so I can be the subject of some damn article."

His jaw clenched and Rina realized she'd stepped over the line—or, at least, he thought she had. The article was the furthest thing from her mind. Without thought, she ran her fingers through his hair, settling her hands in the silken strands. "That's not why I asked."

He cocked his head to one side. "Why then?"

"Because..." How did she explain what she barely understood herself? "Because I've never..." She grappled for the right word. "I've never played that way. With a man, I mean. It's always been pretty straightforward, them doing what they wanted, and it either felt good or it didn't." Her past consisted of a sort of satisfying sex life. Satisfying but nothing like the intensity and steam she was experiencing with

Colin. She shrugged. "I never had the courage to ask for what I wanted."

And no man had ever asked. Another contrast brought to life by Colin. Another place where Colin stood head and shoulders above the rest. In one breath, she wished he weren't so compelling, in another, she thanked her lucky stars she'd found him and they'd share whatever moments fate allowed.

"So, I was wondering. Did you ask what I wanted so you could please me?" She rolled her eyes, embarrassed by her naiveté. "Or because you just liked to hear, oh, I don't know, sex talk? Which I've never done and don't know if I'd be good at. Any more than I'm good at this." She gestured around her. "God, I'm killing the mood, aren't I?"

He laughed, but she sensed he wasn't laughing at her. "Trust me, there's nothing you could do to kill this mood." He grasped her hands and brought them to his lips for a kiss, then he replaced each hand by her side on the counter once more. "You need to know that I asked because I want to please you. But—" His lips twitched and he grinned. "I wouldn't mind hearing some sex talk from *your* lips."

Settled back with her breasts thrusting upward, Rina felt a little wanton—and a lot daring. He picked up where they'd left off, his tongue embarking on another sensual exploration, and her body responded immediately. Hot darts of desire flickered through her.

"Now, tell me what you want." His roughened voice hit her already-sensitized nerves and made her bold.

"I want you to stop teasing me."

In response, his tongue swirled in circles around one nipple, heightening her arousal and causing her body to shake and her hips to pivot back and forth in search of something even more fulfilling than the treatment she was receiving now. But he didn't give in, didn't offer her what she desired. Instead, he just slowly teased her distended nipple, never providing her the relief she sought.

He lifted his gaze, stopping the arousing sensations, and she wanted to cry out in frustration. "Trust me enough to tell me what you want," he coaxed, holding her gaze.

"Take me into your mouth." She struggled for an even breath. "Hold my breast in your hand and take my nipple into your mouth."

His pupils dilated and his eyes burned hot, as hot as the flame he ignited inside her. "Like this?"

He cupped her breast in his palm, kneading the soft flesh and plumping it in his hand.

"Mmm." She leaned her head back and moaned. "More."

And then, finally, he drew her nipple into his hot,

wet, greedy mouth, biting down lightly with his teeth. Alternately grazing, then soothing with his tongue until the fire he lit exploded in a haze of passion. Her hips began gyrating of their own accord. She needed to ease the ache, and he understood.

This time, he didn't wait for her to ask, just lifted her so she could wrap her legs around his waist and thrust the most needy part of her against his thick shaft. Her body soared at their first intimate contact, which felt so good yet wasn't nearly enough. She bucked against him, her hips pushing, writhing, and gyrating into him until her world exploded in a sensational climax she hadn't expected. One unlike any she'd experienced before.

The contractions shaking her body were as strong and vigorous as if she'd taken him inside her. She was still trembling as he set her down on the counter between the sinks. "Oh, God."

He ran a hand through his hair. "That about sums it up." He stepped back and leaned against the flowered wallpaper behind him. "You sure know how to knock the wind out of a guy."

Glancing down, she realized that although she'd been satisfied, he'd been far from it. "Colin…"

He waved a hand in the air, cutting her off. "Don't even suggest it. The first time's going to be the right way, honey. Not with you trying to give me something back just because I made you come."

She blushed at his blunt words, but before she could conjure a reply, he picked up the shirt she'd left on the corner counter, holding it out for her to slip into.

Her heart pounded in her chest and her legs felt like Jell-O as she stood and let him help her dress. As he buttoned her blouse, the act of him dressing her felt more intimate than what he'd just done to her, and the incongruous thought made her smile.

"Something funny?" he asked.

She shook her head. "I'm just thinking."

"About?"

"Just that I picked the right guy to get back into the swing of things again."

He tangled his hands through her hair, groaning as he fingered the tousled strands she'd taken great pains to create. "Why's that?" he asked.

"Because you cared about what *I* wanted. No man's done that for me and it's a gift I'll always remember."

"Rina, I—"

A loud knocking sound interrupted them. "We'll be right out," she called.

Colin clamped his hand over her lips. "I'll," he mouthed, obviously wanting to protect her reputation. "I'll be right out," he whispered.

"I'll be right out," Rina called, a heated blush rising to her cheeks. "Do you think anyone will know what we've been doing?" she asked softly.

"It's Corinne. Emma said I could find Colin upstairs," a familiar female voice called.

He muttered a curse. "I don't want her finding us like this. It's not fair to you."

Rina cared more about how much she liked the sound of *us* rolling off his sexy lips than she did about what Corinne thought. But she appreciated that he cared.

He started for the door she'd thought was a linen closet. "I'll catch up with her in the hall."

"It's about Joe," Corinne called when no one answered her.

"Uh... Colin's in the room next door," Rina replied.

"You get dressed and I'll meet up with you downstairs." He offered her a quick wink and he was gone.

But her body reminded her he wouldn't be forgotten.

HE SHOULDN'T HAVE touched her. Knowing they were on opposite sides, knowing he had to convince Joe to ax her beloved job, Colin should have walked out of the bathroom without looking back. He couldn't, of course. He wanted to be with her too damn badly.

And now that he had, he was shaken. During their intense conversation at the party, they'd connected as though no one else was in the room. Once they were alone, that connection had deepened, both physically and emotionally. When she'd admitted that she'd never asked a man for what she wanted, not even her deceased husband being the implication, Colin had been compelled to put her feelings before his own. He wanted to be the first man she trusted in such an intimate way, and she hadn't disappointed him.

But now, he faced a more difficult truth. Rina was the first woman he was scared to lose.

A knock sounded loud again, drawing him from his thoughts. Buttoning the shirt he'd grabbed from Logan's closet, Colin stepped into the hall to head off Corinne.

"I could hear you banging from in here." He left the bedroom door open so she could glance inside and see he was alone. Although he wished he wasn't... But he meant what he'd said to Rina, and any satisfaction he received wouldn't be found with her hand. "What's wrong with Joe?" he asked Corinne before his damn erection became obvious again.

"He had a ministroke."

Colin's stomach plummeted. This wasn't news he

wanted to hear.

"The hospital called my cell phone and I've been searching all over the house for you."

For a brief minute, Colin softened toward the woman who not only looked extremely upset but who'd bothered to take the time to find him before heading out for the hospital. "Thank you. Can I give you a lift there?" he asked.

She nodded. "I'm too upset to drive."

He grasped her elbow and started for the stairs. Corinne was an enigma, a woman he didn't understand. One minute, her feelings for Joe seemed genuine, the next, she acted erratically without thought for Joe's wishes. Colin groaned, knowing Corinne and his feelings about her weren't important. Joe's health was. "What did the hospital say?" he asked.

"Just that he was stable," she said as they rushed down the long, circular stairs.

He retrieved their coats. "Wait here," he told Corinne.

Colin sought out Emma and Logan to make sure one of them let Rina know why he'd disappeared and covered her ride home. Though he could wait and tell her himself, he didn't want to waste a minute getting to Joe nor did he want to give her some explanation that was bound to be awkward after what had just transpired between them.

He couldn't spare the time to make her feel special and he would have to make it up to her later for leaving. But Corinne had given him an excuse to run now, and he grabbed the chance.

Because Joe's scare came at an opportune moment, at a time when Colin needed space.

He was a man who always left before things became intense, and he didn't know what to do with his craving to be closer to Rina. He felt crowded by his emotions because never in his life had he connected with a woman on such an elemental level.

Rina humbled him. He'd had more invested than just sex in that one encounter, all the while knowing he'd hurt her in the end. Hurt himself as well since losing her was inevitable.

For himself, it was better he build in some emotional distance now. For Rina, it was better she know up front that she couldn't count on him for the long run.

RINA ACCEPTED ANOTHER glass of punch from the server and turned to the good-looking man who'd approached her then proceeded to talk about his portfolio for the last fifteen minutes. He bored her to tears but at least he was paying attention to her.

Unlike Colin, who'd ditched her. He could have

waited and told her about Joe himself or taken her with him to the hospital. He could have done many things. Instead, he'd opted to leave her at the party alone. His actions spoke volumes about something she'd known all along. Colin Lyons was the love-'em-and-leave-'em type. As hurt as she was, she reminded herself she'd wanted a fling, and Colin had just proven he was the right man for the job.

Rina squared her shoulders, determined to make the best of the party and gather information for her column. "So, tell me," she asked Edward Worthington III. "Is your portfolio really as large as you claim?" She leaned in closer and batted her lashes.

He leaned closer. "Come home with me and I'll show you," he said, his implicit meaning obvious.

"Rina already has a ride home," Emma said, grabbing her by the hand and pulling her away. "What do you think you're doing?"

"Research. And tonight, I've discovered that men like outgoing, friendly women."

"Men like to think they'll get lucky, and Edward is out to prove himself ever since his fiancée dumped him because his mother took over their wedding plans. Now, wave goodbye and let him move on to someone who's really interested."

Knowing Emma had a point—she always did—Rina waved goodbye to Edward. She'd only been flirting to take her mind off Colin, anyway. The column was the last thing on her mind.

"Research my patootie," Emma muttered. "You're sulking because Colin left, and that's completely unbecoming."

Rina agreed with the unbecoming part, but since she refused to enlighten Emma as to what had transpired in the bathroom, she clenched her jaw shut tight and followed the older woman into the foyer.

"My driver is ready to take you home," Emma said, patting her hand. "We'll talk more tomorrow when your head is clearer."

"Nonsense. I'll drive Ms. Lowell home." Stan Blecher stepped up beside them. "I heard you tell your driver where she lives and it's on my way home."

"Eavesdropping's rude," Emma muttered.

"So is your attitude, but you don't see me complaining," the older gentleman said.

Rina had never seen Emma put in her place before and bit the inside of her cheek to contain her laughter. "If you're sure you don't mind, I'd appreciate the ride," she said to Stan.

"Of course not. It's been ages since I had someone as young and beautiful as you in the seat beside me." He glanced at Rina and winked. He obviously wanted to make Emma jealous.

"I told you he was a lecher." From the sulking

pout on the other woman's face, his tactic had obviously worked.

"He's a gentleman, Emma," Rina said softly.

"Then let him take you home. I don't give a fig if I ever see him again." With a haughty raise of her chin, Emma pivoted around and walked away. But not before adding, "Colin's a little boy at heart, Rina. Give him the chance to explain."

Rina rolled her eyes because she didn't see her friend giving Stan any chances at all. She met Stan's gaze and shrugged, unsure of what to say now that Emma had taken her leave.

Stan grinned. "Emma lies. Within a week she'll be putty in my hands."

"I hope so." Rina meant her words even more after Stan drove her home.

On the way, he'd told her about the death of his wife, how much he and Emma had in common, and how he just wanted companionship in his later years. Emma, with her outspoken attitude and bubbly personality, suited him fine. Rina agreed. Though she hadn't met Judge Montgomery, only caught sight of the stuffy man from across the room, she didn't think Stan fell into the other man's league. No way would Stan side with Judge Montgomery against Emma. Relieved, she hoped Emma would give in and find the happiness she tried to give others.

Twenty minutes after arriving home, Rina stepped out of her own shower, free of the champagne but not free of Colin or the memory of him bringing her to climax. Alone.

Men. What woman could possibly understand them? At this rate, her series would probably never answer the question.

Towel drying her hair, she glanced at Norton. As soon as she met his gaze, he whined and rolled over onto his back. "At least your needs are simple." She leaned down to scratch his belly when the doorbell rang.

Norton scrambled to his feet and Rina rose, following him to the door. "Coming," she called.

It was 1:00 a.m., late by most standards but early enough for Frankie to stop by for some chocolate-chip ice cream and a chat after her Saturday-night date. This was the first time Rina could contribute to the dating part of the conversation and she needed her friend's advice. "Am I glad to see you," Rina said as she swung the door open wide.

"Well, at least someone is."

Rina winced. "Bad date?"

"The worst." Frankie stomped inside and made herself at home on Rina's couch, propping her cowboy-booted feet so they hung off the armrest without touching the furniture. "How about you? How was your first date since arriving in this quaint New England town?"

Rina closed her eyes and remembered Colin's touch, his warm mouth, and his heady scent.

"That good, huh? Care to tell me your secret?" Frankie grinned.

With her straight inky-black hair, olive skin, and good heart, Frankie shouldn't need anyone's help to find a man. They should be banging down her door. Only they weren't, which made the opposite sex and their desires that much more of a puzzle.

Rina sighed. "No secret to share."

"So, was this a good date or a bad date?"

"Both. I can't say he used me because he certainly didn't get any satisfaction and I did, but he left me at the party and…"

"Whoa. Back up and start over." Frankie's wide-eyed gaze was filled with curiosity.

Rina blushed, realizing what she'd revealed. "Emma spilled champagne on us, and we went upstairs to clean up. Let's just say Colin and I had a moment and leave it at that. But when I arrived back downstairs, I found out he'd received an emergency telephone call and he'd left immediately for the hospital."

Frankie frowned. "So, is he or isn't he a jerk? Tough call."

Rina laughed. "No kidding. He did arrange a ride

home for me," she said in Colin's defense.

Frankie shot her a knowing look. "So, how interested are you in this guy?"

"He makes me feel good." Rina paced the floor in her living room, adrenaline making it impossible for her to relax.

"Which is what you said you wanted in a first-time-out fling."

"Right. Unfortunately, he also really gets to me in here." She tapped her chest, over her heart. "His parents died when he was young, and he's got scars that haven't healed."

"So, he's afraid of being hurt and so are you. Not a bad thing considering you aren't looking for a serious relationship, right?"

When Rina remained silent, Frankie pinned her with a stare. "Right?" she asked again.

"Right. Right," Rina said, hoping by verbalizing the words she'd feel them a bit more. "It's just that he—"

"What?"

She winced. "I feel like I'm being disloyal when I say this, but Colin arouses feelings inside me that Robert never even touched. Physical and emotional." Rina walked to the window and looked out into the snow-covered night. "And that scares me."

"Why?" Frankie asked. "Because if a man did it for me like this Colin guy does it for you, then let me tell you, nothing could keep me out of his bed." She cleared her throat. "I mean life. Nothing could keep me out of his life."

Rina rolled her eyes, but unfortunately, Frankie's point was dead on. "You know what scares me so much? The guy is a guaranteed wanderer. He'll go when this is over." She turned back to face her friend. That fact, which had originally made Colin the perfect man, now put Rina in a frightening situation.

"That just means you have to keep things shallow."

"If it were that easy, I wouldn't be craving chocolate-chip ice cream, now, would I?"

"I thought you'd never offer." Frankie jumped up and headed for the freezer. "Ice cream is a girl's best friend." As she loaded up two bowls, she continued. "There's no problem that I can see. From what you told me, it's been two long years since you've indulged and you're due for some male company. Keep things strictly superficial and you'll be fine. No heartache, no hurt involved."

Exactly what Rina had been telling herself. Unfortunately, everything about Colin was complicated and involved so much more than surface feelings. Before Rina could reply, the jarring ring of her cell startled her. No one ever called at this hour and Rina immediately thought of her parents in Florida. "One sec…"

she said to Frankie, then grabbed for the phone. "Hello?"

"Hey, Rina."

"Colin." Relief settled over her that this wasn't bad news.

"Mmm. Now, *this* is where the night gets interesting," Frankie said.

Rina kicked her in the shin. "Shh," she whispered.

"Hi, honey. Listen, I needed to talk to you," Colin said, his deep voice pulling at her in inexplicable ways.

With his use of the endearment, Rina's mouth grew dry and her nerves kicked in. She lowered herself onto the couch beside Frankie, her legs suddenly unable to support her.

"Did I wake you?" he asked.

"No. I was just entertaining a friend," Rina said, a little devil on her shoulder urging her to bait him.

Because though he'd left for a good reason, there were other ways he could have handled things. Especially after how intimate they'd been minutes earlier. She wasn't angry nor would she hold his ditching her against him. But why not make him wonder?

He cleared his throat. "I see. Well, I just called to make sure you got home safe."

At his concern, her heart skipped a beat. "How's Joe?"

"He had a ministroke. It shouldn't affect him long-term, but it will slow his recuperation and therapy. The doctors are trying to stabilize his medication to prevent it from happening again." He paused. "Thanks for asking."

She heard the pain in his voice and softened, knowing how much he loved the older man. "But he'll be okay?"

"This time. Rina, look. I'm sorry I left you."

His husky voice brought her arousal to life all over again, along with more wariness this time. "I understand."

"Good. Then I won't keep you. I'll see you at work. 'Night, Rina."

"Good night, Colin." She hung up the phone and met Frankie's curious gaze.

"Still unsure of him? Or is it yourself you don't trust?" her friend asked too perceptively. "It's obvious what you want from the guy and it's equally obvious he's interested. He cared enough to make sure you got home okay. Better than my date who left me on the sidewalk and will probably never be heard from again."

Rina rubbed her hands up and down her arms. "I need to take that leap of faith, don't I?"

"No one can answer that except you."

Frankie had a good point, and Rina stood up taller. "You're right. What kind of example do I set for my readers or myself if I overreact and get crazy the first time a guy screws up?"

"I like what I'm hearing."

Rina nodded. "So do I... I know what I want and I know how to go after it."

Frankie applauded and Rina bowed for her audience. But she hoped she could sustain the bravado come Monday morning when she faced Colin again.

Chapter Six

I WAS JUST entertaining a friend. A day later, the comment still stung. After leaving Rina at a party, Colin supposed he deserved the barb. He didn't think she was entertaining a man, but his jealousy had been aroused anyway. Which had probably been the point. He cursed taking the bait.

He had an agenda regarding Rina, but it had been pushed to the back burner by real feelings he hadn't anticipated. Jealousy? Damn.

He picked up the phone and called some smaller companies who advertised in the *Times* and was assured they'd continue to place ads. Then he made preliminary calls to add state and more in-depth national information to the wire service the paper already received. As it was, Corinne was printing what she called "need to know" headlines on an inside section of the paper. Colin jotted notes to contact Bloomberg for financial news and the possibility of acquiring national sports from the AP. Separating man from his sports? It was no wonder Corinne had lost much of her audience. From his perspective, everything was ready to go—should he be able to convince

Corinne in time.

Of course, Colin's changes would cost money, but he'd have to spend something to rebuild readership. Some of that cost could be recouped in Rina's and Emma's salaries, he thought guiltily.

"Good morning, Colin." Emma strode into the office, too perky and happy for a Monday morning. Especially *this* Monday morning.

"Morning, Emma. I take it you spent yesterday resting up from your Christmas bash?" He folded his hands behind his head, happy for the distraction.

"Oh, yes. I soaked in a tub, pampered myself, and read a good book. I'm feeling completely refreshed, thank you. How was your weekend?" She put her purse in her bottom desk drawer as if she'd been here all her life and sat down in her seat.

"I spent yesterday with Joe." And Corinne, but he wasn't in the mood to even think about that now. He was starting to have conflicting feelings toward Corinne, brought on by her constant attention to Joe and his needs.

"Corinne tells me his prognosis is good. I'm so glad." Emma clasped her hands to her chest. "No man should have to spend such a long time in a hospital. I think we should throw him a welcome-back party when he's ready."

This from the woman whose column was on the

line and didn't know it. Colin groaned, needing a reprieve from guilt, pressure, and his own thoughts.

"Delivery," a male voice called, pushing through the doors and entering the offices.

Colin turned to see a man, arms loaded with seasonal flowers.

"I'm looking for a Rina Lowell?"

A low growl escaped Colin's throat at the same time a knot settled in his stomach. Had she had a man in her apartment after all?

"Oh, how exciting. Right here," Emma said, pointing to Rina's desk. Once the flowers were placed on the blotter and the delivery man gone, Emma turned to Colin. "You shouldn't have."

"I didn't," he said through clenched teeth.

Emma raised an eyebrow. "Oh, dear."

Before he could suggest peeking at the card and embarrass himself completely, Rina waltzed inside, a smile on her face, a flush on her cheeks, and her hair tousled from the wind. He got a damn hard-on just looking at her.

"Morning, all." She strode to her desk. "What's this?"

"Flowers, of course," Emma said.

Rina's gaze darted Colin's way for a brief second before she jerked her stare back to the bouquet. But he didn't miss the hopeful glint in her eye and was able to relax. He stepped near her desk and leaned closer so only she could hear. "Sorry, babe. They aren't from me."

"I didn't think they were." She unwrapped the card and read silently, putting the small white envelope in her desk drawer when she was finished.

"So?" Emma asked. "Are you going to share the identity of your secret admirer?"

"They're from Jake and Brianne. Congratulating me on my series starting." Rina didn't meet Emma's gaze when answering, a sure sign something was wrong. But Emma didn't pick up on it.

"That's so sweet. Family's wonderful. Speaking of relatives, I need to make a call and then get to work!" Emma swiveled in her chair, leaving Rina to get settled.

She moved the flowers to the side of the desk, dropped her purse into a drawer, and began to unbutton her wool coat. Colin didn't buy for one minute that her brother and his wife had sent those flowers, but she'd hid the identity of the sender more from Emma than him, which made no sense. He wondered about it for a minute, but when she slid her jacket off her shoulders, the world tilted and all rational thought fled.

Because beneath the oversize coat she wore a black blouse, saved from conservatism by a plunging neckline, and a micro-miniskirt that emphasized her slender legs, which were covered only by sheer, nude-colored pantyhose. At least, he hoped they were pantyhose because if he caught a hint of a lace garter, he'd pass out on sight.

He strode over to her desk, grabbing her hand. "Come with me."

"Where?"

"Coffee break," he muttered, pulling her through the double doors to a stairwell. It wasn't exactly prime office space, but it afforded the only means of privacy he could think of.

Not even the dank smell could dampen his desire or his need to get inside her, body and soul. Once alone, he backed her against the wall, propping one arm over her head. "Who really sent those flowers?" he asked, his baser male instincts coming through.

"You care?"

He rubbed his knuckles down her cheek. "I may have one hell of a way of showing it, but I do."

"Stan Blecher sent the flowers," she admitted.

"What the hell does the old man think he's doing?" Colin asked with a surprised shake of his head.

"The obvious. Trying to make Emma jealous by paying attention to me."

"And you don't want to help his plan?"

Rina rolled her eyes. Men could be *dense* when it

came to matters of the heart. "Of course, I do. But I don't want to hurt Emma. She's not just independent by choice but rather by necessity. She's afraid her son will put her in a home. If she lets herself get close to a friend of his, she fears the same result."

"She said that?"

Rina shook her head. "Insinuated it. And I don't want to be the one to push her into something she's not ready for. Stan admitted he just wants Emma's companionship, but until she can trust him, she's not going to give an inch." Which pretty well summed up any female who'd been hurt or disillusioned by a man, Rina thought.

"So, you're looking out for her."

"That's what friends do," she murmured.

"That's what special, caring people do." His blue eyes bored into hers, causing warmth to blossom in her chest.

After working at her computer all day yesterday and late into the night finishing this week's column, Rina had had it with sweatpants. She'd had it with being alone and she no longer wanted to make Colin sweat. Not in a bad way, anyway. Saturday night was over, and so was her overreaction to Colin's defection. Joe had been in the hospital. Case closed.

So, this morning, she'd dressed with Colin in mind, seeking to grab his attention and not let it go. It had been a girlish impulse and she'd accomplished her goal. But, as usual, Colin had more insight than she'd counted on. He'd looked beyond the physical, deeper than the packaging. He'd seen the woman beneath and obviously admired her.

He tangled his hands in her hair, the erotic tugging sensation rippling through her veins. His admiration and perceptiveness took her off guard. She wanted to keep her barriers high but resisting him was impossible. And when he lowered his head for a deep, leisurely kiss, she wrapped her arms around his neck and kissed him back.

His lips were warm and provocative, taking possession and immediately setting her on fire. No big surprise there. Her tongue met his, swirling, seeking, demanding as much as he gave. And then his hands slipped to her thigh, his large palm branding her. "Do you have any idea what that short skirt does to me?"

"Why don't you tell me?"

"Looking at those long legs makes me hard." He deliberately brushed against her thigh, giving her tangible proof.

She sucked in a breath, her body reacting to the knowledge he wanted her. Here, now, in the dark stairwell, Colin Lyons wanted her. His body backed up his claim and hers went into heated overdrive. Dampness slicked her panties and a rush of desire swamped her.

"And wondering what's holding those things up is driving me insane." Without awaiting permission, his fingers traveled upward until they came in contact with the elastic-rimmed lace that held the stockings up on her thigh. His fingertips hit bare skin and he let out a sharp, harsh breath. "Damn."

She shrugged, trying to act nonchalant. "These are more comfortable."

"For whom?"

She laughed. "For me. Pantyhose cut into my stomach."

"What happened to the baggy clothes?" A muscle ticked in his jaw and Rina knew her new look was getting to him.

But far from enjoying the knowledge, it made her uneasy. Because she wanted to know for sure that Colin was attracted to Rina Lowell, the woman. And though he showed interest in the many facets of her personality, she couldn't deny he was enjoying her transformation.

So had Dave from the coffee shop, who'd turned persistent, and Rob, who'd delivered her pizza last night. She could have had a date with a number of men, including the wealthy Edward Worthington III. But not even in the interest of research could Rina bring herself to go out with anyone other than Colin.

"And what's beneath the skirt?" Colin asked. "What's warming you during this cold, winter weather?"

She was tempted to tell him that she didn't need clothing, not when the heat in his voice could do the trick instead. "Good old-fashioned underwear, Colin, what else?"

An upward sweep of his fingers over her silk-covered sex assured him she was telling the truth. But that same motion set off fireworks inside her brain and triggered mini-explosions, the equivalent of minefields in strategic areas of her body. Her nipples peaked, aching for his touch, and her sex pulsed between her legs. "You don't play fair," she whispered.

"Dressed like that, neither do you." His mouth hovered over hers.

Her lips parted, craving another kiss, but he gave more than she asked for as his finger found the pulse point between her legs. Arousal washed over her, and she jerked her hips forward, seeking to deepen the pressure of his fingertip.

"That works for you, huh?" Resting his cheek against hers, he leaned his body forward, thrusting his hand harder against the tiny pearl of desire begging for release.

"Oh, yes." Her lips lingered against his skin as she inhaled his masculine scent and her desire peaked higher.

This game they played would drive her to distraction if she wasn't careful. She squeezed her thighs together, allowing one last tide of arousal to sweep through her before ducking beneath his arm and gaining space. She needed more time.

He seemed to understand and let her go, studying her in the darkened stairwell as if he could read what she was feeling in her expression. Rina knew exactly why she'd put distance between them, but she wasn't willing to verbalize her thoughts just yet.

While writing her column on attitude, she'd come to a major realization. Looking good meant nothing if a woman didn't feel good about herself. A woman couldn't attract a man let alone keep him happy if she wasn't happy within herself.

Translated into her own life, once she'd quit work and given in to Robert's choices in decor and friends—among other things—spunky Rina Lowell had all but disappeared. She no longer threw on a T-shirt and ripped denim shorts and walked through New York City street fairs nor did she shop the Village for unique but cheap jewelry that would stand out because of its flair. She quit going to the happening clubs where she'd nurse a drink and dance until her feet hurt. Instead, she got old before her time, giving up her fun friends in favor of her husband's staid ones, exchanging nights out on the town for fundraising galas. She'd even altered the way she dressed in order to gain Robert's nod of approval.

She may have looked good in her designer clothes, but she'd slowly lost her inner spark and drive. No wonder he hadn't taken her seriously when she'd expressed interest in writing or doing something outside the confines of their marriage.

Robert thought a credit card would keep her happy, and eventually, she stopped doing anything to convince him otherwise. Because he was giving her a dream life. Too bad it hadn't been *her* dream. She loved him, but she was beginning to doubt they'd have had staying power. The lesson she'd taken away from her latest article, "Strut Your Stuff," was that she now respected herself too much to settle for a man who didn't believe in her, her goals, or her dreams.

Not even for a brief affair. She already knew Colin approved of her work. He'd hinted as much at Emma's party. But before she'd give in to his seductive charm completely, she had to know he accepted everything about her.

"Come dancing with me," she said on impulse. "Friday night."

He leaned against the wall, still holding her gaze. "Dancing?"

"Are you game? I thought I'd check out the Boston nightlife." She needed to recapture the fun she'd been missing, and she wanted Colin to be part of it.

He shrugged. "Why not? Someone has to watch out for you." His lips twitched as he held back a grin.

"I don't need a keeper."

He shook his head, amusement and seriousness warring in his expression. He ran his hand down her neck and dipped his finger into her cleavage, causing her blood to run hotter.

"Something tells me your brother wouldn't agree."

"Low blow." Accurate, she thought, but low. "Jake's a reasonable guy."

Colin's eyes held a wealth of certainty. "Even when it comes to his baby sister?"

"Even then," she lied and crossed her fingers behind her back. "So? Do we have a date? Or am I flying solo?" She wasn't looking forward to nursing a drink and either fending off men or uncomfortably wondering why none approached her. Neither option held any appeal.

Spending time with Colin, however… That prospect appealed to her greatly.

He met her gaze, studying her in an unnerving way. "Why do I feel like you're testing me?" he asked. "And how do I know if I'll pass?"

She was testing herself, Rina mused. *Her* reactions, *her* judgment. "You'll know," she said, her voice husky with anticipation.

"Then we have a date. Since I know the roads, how about I pick you up? Actually, how about we bring Logan and Cat along?"

"As chaperones?" she teased, liking the idea of spending time with his friends.

He grinned. "For fun."

"Sounds good to me."

A loud knock sounded on the other side of the stairwell door. Colin shot her a regret-filled look and stepped toward the door. Freedom, she thought and sighed.

"Rina Lowell, you get out here now," Emma's distinctive voice called to her.

"Some matchmaker," Colin said wryly.

Rina grabbed for the handle. "I'll go out ahead. That will give you some time to calm down," she said with a pointed look at the bulge in his pants.

He shot her an annoyed look. "Very funny," he muttered, but he didn't argue when she let herself back into the hall.

"What's wrong, Emma?"

The older woman waved the white florist card under her nose. "You're being wooed by the lecher." Emma perched her hands on her hips and stared, daring Rina to disagree.

"You mean Colin?" she asked too innocently.

"You mean Colin?" Emma parroted. "Very funny. Stan's sending you flowers. I told you the man was a lecher. Proclaiming his interest in me one minute, showering you with roses the next."

"They're wildflowers, not roses."

"Same difference."

"Not in price," Rina said. "And you were snooping." She snatched the card out of Emma's hand.

"And your lipstick's smudged, which means you were fooling around. How many men are you juggling, anyway?" The older woman sniffed, and Rina stifled a laugh.

Placing an arm around Emma's shoulders, Rina led her back inside and to her chair before easing her into her seat. "You, Emma Montgomery, are jealous. *J-E-A-L-O-U-S.* Because Stan's showing interest in someone else after you turned him down."

"Ridiculous."

"Correct," Rina challenged. "And you know good and well Stan's a smart man. He knows you work beside me, knows you can't keep your eyes or ears to yourself. And he knows you'll find out he sent me flowers and work yourself into a frenzy. Which you did." She clucked her tongue at her elderly friend. "Tsk, tsk, Emma. You shouldn't be so predictable. Men need a woman to be fickle and impulsive." Unable to help it, Rina burst out laughing. "Come on,

Emma. Just go out with the man."

"What if it's a setup?"

Rina understood what her friend meant. What if her son, the infamous Judge Montgomery, had asked Stan to keep an eye on Emma? And what if she was her usual, capricious, whimsical self and her son used it against her? "I can't imagine a son of yours could be so underhanded." Realizing how many stunts Emma had pulled in the name of matchmaking, Rina shook her head. "Scratch that. But I can't imagine he'd be that cruel. Besides, Logan wouldn't let that happen." She patted Emma's hand. "Stan is a lonely widower. And you're in need of the same companionship."

No matter how old Emma was in years, she was young in heart and spirit. And she deserved to have some happiness in her later years.

"Give Stan a chance," Rina said.

"If you do the same," Emma challenged, a gleam in her warm, blue eyes.

"Excuse me?" Somehow Emma had caught her unprepared.

"You open your mind to Colin, and I'll do the same for the lecher."

"His name's Stan, and you'd better remember that before you call him that horrible name to his face."

Emma shook her head. "Quit changing the subject."

"Which is?" Rina asked.

Emma leaned closer, whispering so only Rina could hear. "It's simple. You trust, I'll trust." The older woman shrugged.

Colin chose that moment to reenter the room. Both her body and her heart reacted, proving that when it came to Colin, nothing was simple. Everything was up for grabs. Including, she feared, her heart.

IN ANOTHER ATTEMPT to initiate changes at the *Times,* Colin sat in Logan's office, located on the waterfront overlooking the ocean. Even in the wintertime, the view took his breath away. The weather had been cold, snow covered the ground, and ice replaced the formerly frothing and churning waves.

"Sorry, I had a phone call that ran long. How are you?" Logan strode into his office and shut the door behind him.

"Surviving." Colin clasped his friend's hand and sat back in his chair.

"So, my secretary tells me this is a business visit. What can I do for you?" Instead of sitting behind his desk, Logan joined his friend in one of the guest chairs.

His down-home charm was what the world loved about Logan Montgomery, Colin thought. He shook his head. "You would have made a fine politician, you know."

"And made myself miserable in the process. Nothing's worth that, my friend." Reaching over, Logan grabbed for a picture on his desk and turned it facing them. "Now, *this* is what gets me up in the morning."

A picture of his wife, Cat, their son, Ace, and infant daughter, Lila, on a beach blanket stared back at Colin.

"You are one lucky son of a bitch."

Logan inclined his head. "Find the right woman and you will be, too."

Colin shifted in his seat. He wasn't in the mood to discuss women, not when he was bound to hurt the one he wanted most. The other day, in the stairwell, he'd felt Rina, her arousal on his hand. He'd wanted to be inside her body and let the intense friction they'd created make them both come. He'd wanted to look into her eyes and see that overwhelming sense of trust and goodness. Thank God she'd ducked out on him first. Two days later and he was still thrown, torn by obligation and a growing sense of caring he hadn't expected.

"I need a legal opinion," Colin said, changing the subject.

Logan inclined his head. "Shoot."

"If I were to challenge Joe's power of attorney, the

one leaving Corinne in charge of the paper—which is about to turn into a sinking ship—as Joe's adopted son, can I win?"

Logan exhaled loudly and leaned one foot against his desk. "You don't waste any time, do you?"

"Any reason why I should?" Colin ran a hand through his hair in aggravation.

"What about Joe's wishes?" Logan asked.

No one knew Colin or understood his relationship with Joe better than his former college roommate. Without stepping on Colin's toes, Logan wanted to know if Colin had dealt with the fact that Joe had deliberately and purposefully bypassed his son in favor of his wife. "Until I hear otherwise from Joe, I'm going to assume Corinne got to him in some way."

"Brainwashed?" Logan asked wryly.

"Used sex to get what she wanted. As far as I'm concerned, it's the same thing."

He nodded. "Well, you've already nailed your primary legal problem. Unless you can *prove* that Joe's power of attorney was signed under duress or that he wasn't aware of his actions at the time of signing, Joe's wishes remain."

"So, I don't have a legal leg to stand on?"

Logan shook his head. "Not unless you want to go head-to-head with Corinne in a nasty, expensive court battle."

"That neither the paper nor I can afford." Frustration washed over Colin, along with the first vestiges of anger at Joe, for all purposes *his father,* for betraying him. Anger he hadn't accepted or dealt with just yet. How could he, when doing so would cut himself off from the only family he had?

As it was, Colin fought the urge to run from the situation and let Corinne cope with the consequences on her own. For the first time, his feelings kept him someplace instead of driving him away. His feelings for Rina.

"I think it's time you and Joe talked. Is he up to it yet?" Logan asked.

"After that second stroke, they want to keep him stress-free. But he's doing well and should be up to talking soon."

"Well, whenever you get the green light from his doctor, I suggest you do just that." Logan leaned forward in his seat. "As a friend, I'm going to put myself out there on this one."

"Go on." Colin waited.

"I understand that Fortune's is breathing down your neck, and if you don't get Corinne back on track, the paper will fold. But I've known you for years, and my gut tells me there's something else going on. Something more personal between you and Joe." Logan raised an eyebrow Colin's way.

He flinched because Logan had hit a nerve. "I was always grateful I didn't have a pain-in-the-ass brother."

Logan laughed. "Then you met me. You're talking to the expert on parental grief and aggravation. All I'm saying is that I think Joe's betrayal is bothering you a hell of a lot more than Corinne's change in format." At Colin's glare, Logan added, "Or at least equally as much. Talk to Joe. Then, if you still want to go ahead with any kind of lawsuit, you know I'm on your side. It's just that it'll get messy and probably destroy your family."

"Thanks," Colin muttered. Knowing his friend meant well, he stowed Logan's advice in the back of his mind. "And you don't have to worry. I'll make sure Emma has a job no matter which direction this mess goes." The least he could do was guarantee Emma a return to her desk job, even if she did have to lose her column.

Logan slapped Colin on the back. "Thank you. You know, if she's at loose ends, the Judge will go back to plotting her relocation to an old-age home."

So, Rina's hunch was right, Colin thought. Another reason weighing against him. His head pounding, Colin rose, ready to go over to the hospital.

"How is Rina?" Logan asked, taking him off guard.

"Who?" Colin asked, but a grin came easily despite the gut-churning circumstances. Dammit, the woman made him smile, regardless of what was going on in his life.

"That answers that question. But it doesn't deal with what'll happen to her job if you have your way."

Unwilling to deal with that yet, Colin focused on a more immediate issue. "Are you and Cat busy Friday night? You could get a sitter for the rugrats and come clubbing with Rina and me."

Logan rubbed his hand over his eyes. "It's been forever since we've gone out like—"

"Single people?" Colin asked. But despite his ribbing, a part of Colin envied what Logan had. A wife he loved, kids, a family.

Colin's childhood had been shattered when his parents died. And though Joe and Nell had given him everything, a part of him had always felt as though something was missing, something that would fill an empty part of his soul.

He'd traveled far in search of that elusive thing, to no avail. Now, he'd come back home and was faced with a telling question. Was it possible one woman could complete him?

It was a tall order for anyone to fill. As tall as saving Rina's job and Joe's paper.

Chapter Seven

I T WAS FRIDAY night in Boston, the weekend before Christmas, and this particular club was hopping. The dance floor was full, the bar packed, yet Logan's wife, Catherine, had managed to snag them a table because she'd arrived early.

"So, when do I get to meet this girlfriend of yours?" Cat asked Colin. Her green eyes shimmered with curiosity. "I was so busy avoiding a business crisis at the family party, I missed meeting her. So? Where is she?"

"You always were persistent, Cat. She'll be here. She had a business meeting first." 'Something suddenly came up,' Rina had told him, so instead of Colin picking her up, she was meeting him here.

"Mmm. She works hard." Cat glanced at her watch as Logan studied his wife, a combination of adoration and amusement in his gaze. "Newspaper business at nine-thirty on a Friday night?"

"I don't know. She didn't say what she had to do." And that drove Colin insane, which he figured had been Rina's point. To build the anticipation between them. That or to get even with him over leaving her last Saturday, though he had to admit she seemed to be over it.

"She didn't say why she'd be late?" Cat raised an eyebrow. "Then let me inform you. She wanted to make an entrance." She nodded her head. "Yep, Rina wants to impress you, so she plans to walk in fashionably late."

Colin waved a hand in the air, dismissing the idea. "You don't know Rina." She was up-front and honest about her intentions, something Colin admired.

"And you obviously don't know women." Cat glanced over his shoulder, then leaned forward in her seat, warming to the subject. "Didn't you read Rina's column? She talked about sex appeal. She said women like to be noticed and she's right. Especially in the beginning of a relationship when things are uncertain. No woman wants to be easily forgotten, so it's important to make that impression. What better way than to sashay in a little late, looking amazing?"

"This week she said that attitude is equally important," Logan added.

"You've been reading her column?" Colin asked his friends.

Logan nodded sheepishly, and Colin wasn't sure if his embarrassment stemmed from the fact that he was aware of Colin's intentions for the column or because he'd been caught reading a relationship article.

"All my employees have been reading 'Hot Stuff.' Rina's making quite a name for herself in our little town," Cat said.

Colin couldn't help feeling proud of Rina and wondered if he could use the column's popularity in his favor to get the advertiser to extend that January first deadline.

"Anyway," Cat said. "I think she's taking her own advice. And you have to admit, it's a flattering notion for you. A woman wanting to make you sit up and take notice."

Colin shook his head, disagreeing. "Rina doesn't have to work to impress me."

Logan laughed. "Out of curiosity, if she did make an effort, you wouldn't hold it against her, would you?" He glanced around.

Colin followed his stare and there stood Rina, decked out in a sleeveless red wool dress and matching stiletto heels, doing exactly what Cat had said she would. Making one hell of an impression—on him, and if the other patrons' stares were any indication, on every male in the room.

He couldn't wait to see her, and he'd promised himself he'd put the paper out of his mind and just enjoy the weekend. If Rina's outfit was any indication, she had the same intention. And already his body was reacting to her gorgeous appearance. He wanted her and hoped like hell tonight would be the night.

✧　✧　✧

RINA WANTED TO make an entrance. Corinne's last-minute meeting had helped her do just that. Even better, Rina was still riding an adrenaline wave from her boss's news. Reader reaction to the first few issues of "Hot Stuff" had been phenomenal, surpassing Corinne's expectations. Giddy, Rina was beginning to believe in herself and her ability to make this new career succeed.

She *knew* her positive attitude transferred into the glow in her cheeks, the straightening of her posture, and the excitement rushing through her veins. Okay, so did the anticipation of seeing Colin.

All three people at her table turned her way. Drawing a deep breath, Rina walked over. "Hi, everyone. Sorry I'm late, but I had a meeting with Corinne." She settled into her seat, aware that Colin's gaze hadn't left hers. Or rather, hadn't left her body, which had been her plan.

The fact that he'd brought his friends along told her he was letting her into his life in a way that surpassed the superficial, something she realized she'd needed in order to take that next step with him. He'd accepted her, and that was enough to allow her to act on the desire that had been growing between them.

Colin rose, as did Logan.

"And they say chivalry is dead," Rina joked. She settled in more comfortably beside the woman who had to be Catherine. Rina had caught glimpses of her rushing around at the Christmas party, but they hadn't officially met. "I'm Rina Lowell."

"Catherine Montgomery."

The blonde, who Rina would love to hate for her beautiful face and perky disposition, smiled, making her feel welcome.

"I've been dying to meet you," Catherine said. "But I was running around like a crazy person at the party. I'm so glad you invited us tonight. And now, I guess I should shut up and let you talk." Catherine grinned.

Rina laughed. "Colin's said wonderful things about you. It seems like he was right."

Catherine shook her head. "The man's a charmer. He'd say anything that suited him."

Beneath the table, Rina felt someone kick their foot out hard.

"Ouch," Cat muttered. "Sorry. I have a big mouth. I meant that Colin is a charmer of the best kind. I'm really shutting up now." She deliberately clenched her jaw tight.

Rina laughed again. "Don't worry. I know who and what Colin is." Her gaze met his and the fire she saw burning there warmed her inside and out.

They shared an enjoyable round of drinks and appetizers, Rina learning she could judge a lot about a man by his friends. Whereas Robert's friends were colleagues, stuffy attorneys more full of themselves than she could bear, Logan was the opposite. Warm and fun like his grandmother. In his eyes, Rina saw Emma's spunk and mischievous nature. She also saw that both he and Catherine cared for Colin, treating him more like family than a friend.

Another half-hour later, the check was paid and Colin had moved closer, his thigh brushing her nearly bare one beneath the table. The short dress had hiked up her legs and his warmth caused a sizzling in her veins. She wanted him more than she'd ever wanted a man. She needed to explore this thing between them and let the passion explode.

"Would you like to dance, Rina?" Logan asked. "My wife made me swear I wouldn't make her spend any more time on her feet than necessary. She'll be working parties and running around for the rest of the weekend."

The background music suddenly became clearer, a throbbing beat made more intense by the pulsing inside her body, the longing she felt for Colin alone.

But since she didn't want to be rude, she agreed to a dance. She and Colin had the night to be together, or so she hoped.

She and Logan moved onto the floor and danced through two songs. Rina enjoyed Logan's sense of humor and wit. Unfortunately, he wasn't Colin, and she wished the last song would end so she could be in Colin's arms. So he could pull her close enough to feel the heat of his body and inhale the heady scent that aroused her and made her wet with wanting him.

Finally, the music ended, and Logan stepped back. "Before we go to the table, I wanted to tell you something."

"What's that?"

"There's something about Colin you may not know. I roomed with the guy in college. He doesn't bring the women he dates around his friends. Even before Julie, he was wary."

"Who's Julie?"

"That's for Colin to tell you." Logan winked. "I'm just trying to let you know that you're special to him."

"Your wife's getting jealous," Colin said, coming up beside them.

Rina glanced back at the table. Catherine had ordered another drink and was talking to the waitress, oblivious to anything happening on the dance floor, making Colin's claim a blatant lie.

Rina swallowed a laugh because there was nothing funny about Colin's possessiveness. The emotions said a lot for his feelings, backing up Logan's claim. "Are you interrupting us for Cat's sake? Or for your own?" Rina asked, finished playing games.

"I think this is my cue to disappear." Chuckling, Logan leaned over and whispered in Rina's ear. "He doesn't bring women back to his place, either." Then he slapped Colin on the back and made his way to the table and his wife, waving goodbye from a distance as he helped Catherine on with her coat.

Alone on the dance floor, Rina looked into Colin's heated gaze and shivered.

"I don't want you to be cold."

"Then warm me," she said, taunting him. Daring him. Begging him, she thought.

But instead of dragging her into the nearest dark room and having his way with her as her fantasy dictated, he pulled her into his arms. His body aligned with hers, and beneath her dress, her nipples puckered as desire licked between her legs and an overall sensual tug of need swamped her.

The dance floor was crowded, but they might as well have been alone as they swayed from side to side. Music beat out a heavy, carnal sound, matching the rhythm quaking inside her.

"Warmer?" he asked at last.

"Mmm," she purred as his lean, hard body took her on the beginning of what she hoped would be a very sensual ride. She inhaled, savoring the masculine scent of his cologne, letting him seep inside her pores and her skin.

"Rina?"

She tipped her head backward, forcing her heavy eyelids open. "Yes?"

His thumbs brushed over her lips, letting her dampness coat his fingertips. The sensations as he caressed her mouth overwhelmed her and she swallowed a moan.

"Do you want to get even hotter?"

His voice took on a low, husky quality that reverberated over her already-sensitized nerve endings. She couldn't mistake his meaning. She already knew she wanted the night to end in bed.

Meeting his gaze, she nodded but didn't feel anything like the courageous wanton she pretended to be. "I want to burn."

"Then what are we waiting for?" His hand in hers, he led her off the dance floor, silent understanding about what was to come surrounding them.

By driving into Boston with Corinne, she'd left herself free to return home with Colin. On the long car ride, Rina had a lot of time to reflect on the woman she'd become around Colin. She'd never been so brazen before, not in thought or deed. But no other man had ever allowed her such freedom to be herself.

None had ever seen her playful side. She bit her lip and glanced out the car window. The white snow in contrast to the jet-black night made her think of the woman she was... and the woman she'd been. These days, she'd returned to being the Rina whose ideal Christmases as a child had been spent playing in the snow, then warming up with hot cocoa at the kitchen table.

Colin respected that woman. Colin, a man who'd taken one look at her outrageous red dress and rather than disapprove, he'd drooled and even grown jealous. She studied his handsome profile. Just the sight of him quickened her pulse and a ripple of excitement darted through her.

She clenched and unclenched her fists, all too aware of the fact that with Colin, she felt not just accepted but alive.

One hand on the steering wheel, he met her gaze. Need flared in his eyes and found an answering heat in hers.

She squirmed in her seat, desperate for a distraction. "Mind if I turn on some music?" she asked.

"My place is closer," he said at the same time.

They'd agreed to be together. They hadn't discussed where. *He doesn't bring women back to his place,* Logan had said. The beating of her heart echoed in her ears in the confines of the small car. "Is that an observation or an invitation?" she asked, needing to keep things light. Needing an answer even more.

He laughed. "You don't play games. I respect that about you." He reached over, his hand touching, then covering hers.

Heat seared her already-sensitized skin.

"It's an invitation," he said. "One I don't extend lightly."

He met her gaze once more, hunger and more than she was ready to deal with shimmering in the darkened depths.

She drew a deep breath before answering. "I accept. And it's not something I do lightly, either."

His hand squeezed hers, his thumb caressing her skin. He turned off the highway an exit earlier than her own. Two or three short turns later and he drove into a gated town house complex. Lit only by streetlamps and the occasional room occupied by a night owl, they were enveloped in a cocoon of darkness that fit the wanton, decadent way she was feeling.

Staring out the car window, Rina couldn't get a mental image of the development where Colin lived. She'd have a better idea come morning.

Oh, wow.

She stepped out of the car and glanced up. When had it started to snow? She'd been too preoccupied with her thoughts to notice. Needing the release, she spread her arms out and twirled around, letting the flakes hit her face and the wind whip around her until Colin pulled her into his arms.

"You're the ultimate snow bunny." Serious and intense as she'd ever seen him, he dipped his head for a lingering kiss, one hot enough to melt the snow around them. His mouth sizzled against hers. She'd come here for one reason only, and he obviously intended to give her what she wanted.

By the time he took her hand and led her inside, awareness and desire had all but overwhelmed her. But she had no reservations, no doubts. She was ready.

✧   ✧   ✧

COLIN WATCHED AS Rina shrugged off her jacket, revealing the sexy dress that had tied him up in knots all evening. He reached out for her coat then dropped it onto the couch beside his. "You know, if it wasn't for the snow on the ground, we'd never have made it inside."

"And why's that?" Mischief twinkled in her eyes.

Sexy mischief he couldn't resist. "As if you don't know. I want you so badly, the walk from the car to the house was pure torture."

She threw her shoulders back and strutted toward him. There was no other word for her deliberately provocative movements. She meant to inflame his senses and she accomplished her goal beautifully.

"Then what are we doing wasting time talking?"

"Damned if I know." She'd tasted delicious and he wanted more. Reaching for her shoulders, he brought her flush against him, sealing his lips against hers and sealing the inevitable outcome at the same time.

A purring sound rose from her throat and reached inside him. His lips traveled to her cheeks, following a moist path down her neck and pausing to nibble on her bare, luscious throat. He inhaled and smelled pure femininity, pure Rina, and a burst of desire shot through him.

Her head tipped backward, affording him better access, and he took advantage, licking and nibbling at her flesh. "I want to feel you naked," she murmured. "Skin against skin, I need to know what your body feels like against mine."

He smiled. This was what he liked best about Rina, the surprises. Demure and quiet on the car ride home, tigress now.

Pulling her closer, he brought her against him.until his hard erection pressed fully into the vee of her legs, he shut his eyes and savored the intense feeling. "You'll fit perfectly."

"Then let's get naked and see," she said impishly, a blush on her cheeks and a smile on her face.

He didn't need a second invitation. He reached for

the short hem of her dress at the same time she did and together they pulled the garment up and off. She was a vision in red—red bra, red panties, all sinfully decadent. "I've died and gone to heaven."

"Care to take me with you?"

"Hell, yes." He was harder than he'd ever been and he gritted his teeth, unbuttoning his denim shirt. But before he could finish, she grabbed onto the material and ripped the shirt down and off his shoulders.

"Slow has its time and place, Colin. But now's not it."

He agreed and reached to unhook her bra. If he thought she was incredible in all that lace, she was even more superb without it. Her breasts were plump and enticing, her nipples peaked and ready as she stepped toward him. She let her fingers travel to the waistband of his pants, and next thing he knew, he was kicking the trousers aside.

She bit her lip in intense concentration, gazing downward at his straining erection begging for relief, near to bursting against his boxer briefs.

When she deliberately let her hand graze over the bulge in his pants, Colin's restraint vanished. Moving quickly, he backed her to the couch, tossed the clothes onto the floor, and came down on top of her on the black leather sofa. Her body was soft, supple, and pliant beneath his; her warm, wet sex cradling him in heat.

His mouth met hers, the kiss ravenous, a release of all the pent-up sexual tension they'd been creating all week. She tasted of wine and Rina and he couldn't get enough. His tongue thrust into her waiting mouth as he mimicked the movement with his hips, jerking forward, getting as close as possible without entering her willing body. That would come.

At the moment, their bodies were in sync as well as their minds. He opened his eyes in time to see her watching him, eyes glazed with desire and a depth of emotion that would have shaken him if he wasn't feeling it himself. For days now they'd danced around each other, feeding the mutual need and teasing one another with erotic touches and silent promises. With foreplay.

His body shook with the need to keep those promises now.

Taking him off guard, she wrapped her legs around his back, and ground her body in an enticing circular motion against his. The wave beckoned slowly, building to a heated crescendo that could have but one resolution.

No way in hell was he coming without being inside her. Neither, he swore to himself, would she.

"Condoms are in the bedroom," he managed to say, hoping like hell he wasn't killing the mood.

"They're also in my purse on the floor next to you." Despite the intimacy of their position, a flush rose to her cheeks.

She was obviously embarrassed that she'd been so anxious, and the fact that she wasn't proficient at this made her all the more endearing. He stroked her cheek with the back of his hand, wanting her to know she was special.

"Colin?"

"Mmm?"

"I'm on the pill and haven't been with a man since my husband." She paused, then shook her head. "What I'm trying to say is… I'm safe."

He inhaled deep. He'd never made love to a woman without protection, never wanted the responsibility a mistake could cause. He'd contemplated the notion with his wife. Marriage had him thinking of family in the traditional sense, but Julie hadn't been eager to lose her figure. Another thing they should have discussed before tying the knot. After her departure, he'd applauded her selfishness since it left him with no permanent ties to a woman he considered nothing more than a mistake.

Rina was different. In every way. "I'm safe, too," he admitted.

"You don't feel safe," she said, squeezing her thighs tighter, intensifying the spiraling sensations. She lay her head back and moaned, and the thought of being inside her with no barriers between them, nothing except melding flesh, made him burn hotter. To hell with the consequences, with the problems lying ahead of them.

To hell with everything but this. He pulled the thin string holding her panties until the material tore in two, and tossed the garment on the floor, giving Colin a view of perfection.

"Sweet heaven," he muttered. He moved aside long enough to pull off his boxer briefs and drop them to the floor, then noticed she'd changed positions. Against the black sofa she lay, legs spread wide, waiting. For him.

He came over her, his hands grasping her thighs at the same time his thumbs caressed and parted her silken, damp flesh. Her breath caught in her throat, her pleasure unmistakable.

"This works for you?" He ran a finger over her slick heat, slipping inside.

"Oh, yes." Her hips jerked upward in silent acknowledgment, taking him in deeper.

At the simulation of sex, a shudder wracked his body, making him feel as out of control as he'd been when he was a teenager. But no, he thought. This was far worse because no other woman had ever affected him this way.

And Rina hadn't been with anyone since her husband. The thought both sobered and humbled him. He wanted to give her perfection. He wanted to give her everything he had.

Nudging himself at her opening, he thrust fast and deep, giving her what *he* needed, what he sensed, she did as well. From her satisfied cry that shook the silent house, he'd been right.

He wanted to savor the moment that had been so long in coming, but they were both too far gone. Her hips gyrated, seeking release, and his body thrust of its own volition, only too happy to comply. Harder, hotter, the slick, synchronized movement between them created not just intense sensation but a swell of emotion he hadn't been prepared to face.

Though he'd known he and Rina wouldn't just have sex, the perfection of the moment completely overwhelmed him. But as she repeated her earlier motion, wrapping her legs around his back and nearly lifting herself off the couch, she brought him so deep into her, he wasn't certain where he left off and she began. And he didn't want to know.

He only wanted to feel, and when she dug her nails into his flesh and let go completely, Colin felt set free.

Chapter Eight

COLIN STRETCHED OUT beside Rina, every inch of his lean, hard, body coming into delicious contact with her skin. His fingers tangled in her hair and he pulled her close. After their encounter on the couch, they'd moved to his bed, where she'd slept more deeply than she'd ever remembered. Being with him had been a mind-altering experience, one she was all too ready to repeat this morning.

But not yet. "Tell me about Julie." Logan had planted the seeds of her curiosity surrounding Colin's past and Rina wanted to explore them. To know more about this enigmatic man who made her come apart so easily.

He groaned. "Hell of a way to start the day," he muttered.

Okay, so it wasn't the best question first thing the morning after, but she'd spent the night in his arms. He'd spent it inside her body. She figured that allowed her some leeway.

"She's my ex-wife." He rolled over and propped up on one arm.

The sheet pulled low on his chest and the urge to

press her breasts against him and drop this whole conversation was strong. Unfortunately, her curiosity was stronger. "And?"

He met her gaze. "She's in the past."

"A painful past?" She probed deeper.

He shrugged. "It only hurts if you care. I'm over it."

"I should hope so, considering where we are."

He exhaled hard, and she knew he was going through that frustrating process of withdrawal.

"So, why do I have the feeling that knowing Julie's in the past isn't enough?" he asked.

"Because I'm a woman and I like to push."

"Even if I'd rather do something more than talk?" A wry, sexy smile tipped his lips.

Good, she thought. He wasn't angry, just attempting to maintain his dignity with stoic silence. She rewarded his patience with her questions with a long, lingering kiss. One that quickly threatened to explode in another session considering they were both still naked. But she wasn't ready to give up on emotional intimacy for more sex, as much as her body craved him.

She broke the kiss, licking at her damp lips. A disheveled Colin was as devastating to her senses as a well-put-together one. And if the man was going to have this kind of effect on her, she needed to understand all about him.

"Did you love her?" Rina asked.

✧   ✧   ✧

COLIN ROLLED BACK and lay a hand over his eyes, resigning himself to talking before any other desires were satisfied. Truth be told, he wanted to confide in Rina, which surprised him since he wasn't a sharing kind of guy.

"Not the way I should have. Then again, the feeling was mutual." Sensing Rina's gaze on him, he stared up at the ceiling, wanting a clear head when he answered her. "I was a news anchor on a local station in Boston when Julie and I met. We had some things in common and I thought she was a refreshing change from the women who wanted the more dominating personality they saw on TV."

"You, dominating?" Rina laughed.

"After last night are you seriously doubting me?" He pushed her onto her back, straddling her hips.

She sucked in a shallow breath. "Definitely not."

"So, do you want to hear about my disastrous marriage, or would you rather repeat some of those erotic positions we tried last night?" He asked, his erection poised at her moist, ready flesh.

She sighed, obviously torn, her wide brown eyes filled with curiosity and desire. He didn't blame her for either. He wanted equal insight into her past and planned to get it after he satisfied his need for her this morning. He doubted he'd ever have his fill of her completely, something he'd have to deal with soon.

"I want you to talk. I want to know all about you. Then I want to have sex."

"Okay," he said, resigned. "Julie and I got married. I was working at the network, restless with the job and life, but that wasn't anything new or different for me." He'd always been restless, ready to move on. So why wasn't he compelled to bolt now, when things in his personal life were at their most complicated? He knew the reason lay in his arms, waiting for more answers. "I think Julie sensed my restlessness. Not that it's an excuse for cheating, but I think she wasn't any happier than I was."

"She cheated on you?" Rina asked.

Realizing he hadn't been clear, Colin laughed. Amazing that she hadn't jumped to the conclusion that *he'd* been the one to stray, which said volumes about her faith in him. Unwarranted faith under the present circumstances, but it pleased him anyway. "Yeah, she did. Obviously, she wasn't getting what she needed out of the relationship."

"Or she didn't know the meaning of truth, honesty, and fidelity," Rina said in disgust.

Ouch, he thought, taking the direct hit. "I think

Julie just wanted me to be satisfied at home and, sensing I wasn't, she went looking elsewhere."

"I never realized we had anything so fundamental in common. My husband wanted me to be more satisfied at home than I was."

"He didn't cheat on you, did he?" Colin wouldn't want Rina to suffer the humiliation.

She shook her head. "I think what he wanted was almost worse. He wanted to change me."

"Foolish man."

Her eyes shimmered with happiness. "That's what I like about you, Colin. You accept me for who I am and respect what I want to do in life." She shook her head. "For as long as we last, I'll know you're not a man who has some wrong vision of who I am or some alternative idea of what I should be doing. You want me."

Yes, he did. For as long as she'd have him and, he feared, beyond. Colin nudged her legs aside with his, and while she watched, he entered slowly. "I want *you*." He thrust deep and she took all of him, arching her hips while her body contracted around him, milking him with her tight, wet heat.

She shuddered and sucked in a breath. "I want a man to know me and accept me."

He withdrew, feeling her swollen and wet surrounding him. "I want to know all of you. Every last thing about you."

She bent her knees, forcing him to thrust deeper in order to maintain body contact. "I want to know you the same way."

"Then what are we waiting for?" he asked and proceeded to know her. Accept her. And she did the same, taking him, accepting every last bit he had to offer.

RINA TURNED ON the shower in Colin's bathroom. She inhaled the scent of shaving cream and aftershave. Colin's aftershave. Just the delicious smell was enough to arouse her sensitive body all over again.

As much as she'd like to head back into the bedroom to repeat the experience, she knew she had to shower and let Colin drive her home. She'd called Frankie and left word for her to walk Norton, but she couldn't be certain her friend had gotten the message. And Norton, the pampered pooch, wasn't used to being alone overnight any more than Rina was used to spending her nights in a man's bed.

Any more than she was used to bonding with a man emotionally, and for that reason, her escape home came at the perfect time. Ironically, this time she needed space and time to think.

And an hour later, Colin drove her home. He

pulled up to the Cape house and she noticed an unfamiliar black car parked in the driveway. "Maybe Frankie's got company."

"Frankie, *your* company?" he asked wryly, reminding her of last Saturday night's phone call.

Rina grinned. "Frankie, my female friend who lives downstairs." She'd told him about Frankie over a quick breakfast of cold cereal in his kitchen, where she'd admitted to baiting him last weekend.

"Wouldn't be unusual for people to have family over during the holidays. By the way, that reminds me of something I've been meaning to bring up. And would have if you weren't so sexy and distracting. Christmas Eve is tomorrow night." He turned off the ignition at the same time he turned on the charm, treating her to the endearing grin she'd come to know so well. "Did you have any plans?"

Jake and Brianne were coming up from New York tomorrow when her sister-in-law got off from work, and she wanted Colin to meet them. She refused to think about what that meant. Neither did she want Colin to be alone while Joe lay in a hospital bed.

But she wanted to hear his thoughts before she sprang her suggestion on him. "What did you have in mind?"

He twirled her hair around his finger. "I noticed there's no Christmas tree in your apartment."

Now that he mentioned it, she'd noticed the same about his condo. "I didn't want to put one up alone." Jake would probably kill her when he arrived and discovered she'd neglected their favorite family tradition, but she hadn't wanted to go tree shopping solo.

"Tsk, tsk," he said jokingly. "Don't you think Norton deserves a festive holiday?"

"Norton!" She had to get inside and let him out. Reaching for the handle, she jumped out of the car and ran up the back stairs.

Once outside her apartment, she paused. A pair of women's slippers sat by the welcome mat in the hall. A pair of wet women's slippers with gold embroidery that could only belong to one person. Rina crinkled her nose, recognizing that Norton had done his business yet again, this time on Emma's shoes. Though what Emma would be doing here, she hadn't any idea.

"Oh, no. Emma? Emma, is that you?"

Colin's footsteps sounded behind her as he followed her inside. "Emma's here?"

Rina pointed to the damp slippers. "No self-respecting prowler would wear these or leave them as evidence. Frankie must have let her in." She ran a hand through her still-damp hair. Colin, guy that he was, didn't have a blow-dryer. "I wonder what she wants."

He groaned. "Does it matter? We get to be inter-rogated by the matchmaker the morning after. That's fun I wouldn't mind missing."

"Chicken." She grinned, grabbed his hand, and pulled him inside, surprised when Norton didn't come bounding toward her. "Emma?" she called once more.

"I'm in the kitchen."

Rina stepped into the room and found Emma, the sleeves of her silk blouse rolled up to her elbows as she rinsed what looked like a pair of pantyhose in the sink.

Norton had obviously ruined them as well as her shoes. Rina winced. "Hi, Emma."

"Hello, dear. Your friend Francesca let me in. Lovely girl. Bad date last night and I'm coming up with a list of possible men to help her out." Emma shut off the faucet and wrung out the damp hose.

"I see you met Norton?" Rina asked carefully.

"Oh, yes." Emma smiled.

"And you aren't angry?"

She shook her head. "What can you expect when the poor thing's been left alone *all night?* You should be happy I don't report you to the ASPCA." Her wink made a mockery of her words.

Rina rolled her eyes. Norton was perfectly capable of holding himself for the time she'd been gone. He had an extraordinary bladder. "What happened?"

"He got so excited when I rang your bell. It was about the same time Francesca had come upstairs to walk him, and while she was looking for the leash, he... uh... well, suffice it to say he didn't quite make it this time." She lifted her shoulder in the delicate shrug Rina had come to know well. "Anyway, Frankie took him for a walk, and she said she'd keep him downstairs for a while. Just in case he had any ideas about repeating himself."

Rina shook her head. "I'll pay for your shoes and pantyhose." Knowing Emma's expensive taste, replacing them would probably set her back a fair penny. But somebody had to pay Norton's debts.

"Never mind that." Emma lay her stockings over one of Rina's kitchen chairs as if she lived there and walked into the living room, expecting them to follow.

Of course, they did.

"You two have some explaining to do," she said as she turned around and seated herself in the club chair in the corner, holding court in Rina's house.

Colin walked by and knelt down beside Emma. As he passed, Rina inhaled his masculine scent and her body heated up all over again. The timing was all wrong, of course. As much as Rina enjoyed Emma's company, the older woman seemed to have taken up residence, hadn't told Rina what she wanted, and didn't seem inclined to leave anytime soon.

After lifting Emma's hand in his, Colin placed a kiss on her hand. "You know I adore you."

Was it Rina's imagination or did Emma actually blush?

"Of course, you do, you charmer, you. It still doesn't mean you don't have some explaining to do, keeping Rina out all night."

"How do you know we didn't just go for breakfast?" Rina asked.

"Because you're dressed like a hot number in wrinkled clothing, which leads me to believe you've been out all night. You can't pull the wool over my eyes. I'm too old and I've been around. Now, young man, what do you have to say for yourself?"

Colin laughed. "Only that I adore you."

Rina walked closer to the chair. "Not that you aren't welcome anytime, but what are you doing here now?"

"That's a good question." Colin rose to his feet and thrust his hands into his back pockets, waiting for an answer.

"Honestly?"

Rina threw her hands in the air in pure frustration. "Of course!" she said on an exasperated breath.

"I came to snoop."

That took Rina off guard. "What?" Last time Emma nosed around, she'd found Stan's card. This time, Rina had nothing to hide.

"I came to have tea, make small talk, excuse myself to go to the ladies' room, and see what evidence you'd left around. Then I realized that you're my dear friend and such behavior is inexcusable. *Not* that you've been looking out for my feelings, but I certainly look out for yours."

Rina's head was swimming. "I don't know what you're talking about." Turning to Colin, she asked, "What is she talking about?"

He merely shrugged, one eyebrow raised as he, too, waited for an explanation.

"Did you know she's two-timing you, Colin?"

"What!" Rina and Colin both asked at the same time.

Emma nodded. "She's giving me competition for my dear Stan."

Rina blinked. "You said the man's a lecher. Now he's your dear Stan? Come on, Emma. What gives?"

"First he sends you flowers." She sniffed, pulling a handkerchief out of the cuff of her sleeve. "Then he asks you out."

"He did no such thing," Rina said, outraged.

Colin coughed, lifting his hand to cover his obvious laughter. The traitor. Rina would deal with him later, but first, there was the matter of an outlandish eighty-year-old storyteller to deal with. "Prove it, Emma."

"Stan showed me a copy of the letter he penned asking you out. Flowery language and written in his own hand."

Rina rubbed her temples. "He's playing you. He never sent any letter. But he wants you jealous and you are. You're interested in the man. Just admit it and go out with him, for heaven's sake." She shot an imploring glance at Colin.

"Emma?" Colin prodded.

Old, wise eyes met Rina's. "I'm afraid."

"Logan won't allow the Judge to put you in an old-age home, Emma," Colin assured her.

He spoke the words Rina had tried to convince Emma of already. But hearing him say it, Rina believed. She trusted Colin's instincts. His judgment. And that meant her feelings for this man went deeper than she'd ever imagined.

She shivered, forcing herself to focus on Emma. "Isn't that the same thing I told you the other day?"

The older woman nodded.

"Life is short," Rina said, speaking from experience. "Please trust me on this and live every day to its fullest. If Stan wants to be your companion, then get to know him. Trust your own instincts."

"I know you're right. I just wish it was easy."

Rina didn't miss the irony in Emma's life. She had no problem trusting her instincts when giving advice to others, but when it came to herself, she doubted her judgment. For the first time, Emma looked fragile, a word Rina had never associated with her before. She wanted to strangle the *judge* herself, but she'd settle for comforting her friend.

As if reading her mind, Colin walked over and pulled Emma into a silent hug. Over Emma's shoulder, he met Rina's gaze. Sizzling heat and understanding passed between them.

Emma rose and cleared her throat. "Well, I plan to give Stan a piece of my mind for deceiving me," she said, back to her old feisty self.

Rina smiled. "I bet you will."

"And I'll be keeping an eye on you, young lady. No more two-timing this wonderful man." With a chuckle, she embraced Rina. "You are a good girl, Rina. I wish I had a daughter like you. And a son like you, Colin."

"You just take care of yourself. More importantly, be good to yourself, okay?" Rina said.

"Am I ever anything but good?" A naughty twinkle settled in Emma's blue eyes. At least she'd brushed off her bout of insecurity. "Now, I believe my driver's waiting in the car."

Rina raised an eyebrow. "I didn't recognize the car. Come to think of it, I didn't see anyone sitting in it, either."

"I borrowed the judge's favorite sedan. Heaven forbid he thinks he has the upper hand." She sniffed. "As for my driver, he probably went to take a leak… er, do his business." She shot Rina a wink and laughed.

Rina chuckled, helping Emma on with her coat and providing her with a pair of flat shoes to wear out to the car. "We'll settle Norton's mess later, okay?"

"Nonsense. It's over and done with. Just give him a kiss for me. I love that boy." And then she was gone.

Exhausted, Rina leaned against the wall and glanced at Colin. Somehow, she found the energy to laugh. "Alone at last."

He grinned. "We certainly are. So, can we get back to discussing Christmas Eve?" Because Colin didn't want to put off asking her to spend the holiday with him one more minute.

She bit down on her lower lip. "I think I'd asked you what you had in mind."

"You, me, a small tree we buy today and decorate, and then sex by the fire all weekend long." His body burned at the thought, and from the inferno in her gaze, she obviously felt the same way.

"It all sounds so great," she said in a husky voice that aroused every male instinct he possessed. "We can do all that for the rest of today and tonight. As for tomorrow, we could have that fire if you don't mind sharing with family."

"Family?"

"Mine. With all the excitement over my series, then my desire to seduce you—"

"You wanted to seduce me?" he asked, obviously joking, obviously pleased as his lips hovered over hers.

His scent, his heat all worked to get her all stirred up again. "Stop and let me finish. I was so distracted, I forgot that Brianne and Jake are coming tomorrow."

Disappointment hit him hard. He'd counted on Rina's brother being out of state, on his and Rina's similar lack of family to push them together for the holiday. So much for the intimate night he'd planned. "I wouldn't want to intrude on a family holiday."

A wounded look crossed her face. "Who said you'd be intruding? I just invited you. I would have asked you to stay anyway had I remembered they were coming. You just kept me too distracted to think clearly." She stepped toward him, a come-hither look in her eyes, a sizzling, sexy smile on her lips. "It wouldn't be a holiday for me without you."

She trailed her fingertips up his chest, letting them linger on the collar of his sweater. She knew how to get to him in word and deed. Heat pervaded his body, and a throbbing erection took up residence in his jeans. And when she stepped closer, letting her chest brush against him, the swell of her breasts gave him every indication her invitation was sincere. Family or no family, he supposed he could deal with it.

For Rina, he could probably cope with anything.

"How about you go down, get Norton, do whatever you need to around here, and then we go tree shopping?"

"Does that mean you'll be here when Jake and Brianne arrive?"

"As long as you keep Norton away from my shoes, I'll do anything you ask."

"Anything?" she asked with a grin.

"You're naughty, Rina."

"And you love it."

He nodded. He sure as hell did. And the notion caused his chest to constrict.

"Give me half an hour to get Norton and change and then I'm all yours," Rina said. After brushing a kiss over his lips, one that was brief but electric, she bolted for Frankie's.

Cheeks flushed and glowing, she lit up something inside him. Colin never wanted to lose the feeling, but he warned himself not to get too used to it. Life was all about change. His parents' deaths, Joe and Nell taking him in, his brief marriage, followed by Nell's death, Colin's divorce, and then Joe's marriage to Corinne. Nothing ever stayed the same.

Fate always threatened to take away what he loved

most. But in this case, Colin himself had the means to tear him and Rina apart. But he hoped to build a solid foundation before then, something that could withstand the repercussions when they came.

Chapter Nine

AROUND FOUR THAT afternoon, Colin lugged a pathetic-looking tree up Rina's stairs. "This thing looks like it's seen better days."

Rina unlocked the door and held it open so he could drag their tree inside. "We're lucky they had any left the day before Christmas Eve. Personally, I don't care what it looks like. It's ours and that's all that counts."

Norton barked when they entered, and he danced around, jumping on Colin with his front paws. "Go walk him before I become his next victim, will you?"

Rina laughed. "I expect that tree set up and ready to be decorated when I return."

"Slave driver." He winked and waved her away.

A few hours later, he stepped back to admire their handiwork. The small tree twinkled with all the spark, spunk, and spirit that Rina had brought into his life. Red, green, and gold ornaments decorated the branches, along with silver tinsel and a shiny star on top. The result was commercial in color but warm and comforting in the aura it exuded. A fire crackled in the small fireplace where Norton lay basking in the heat before deciding to snooze on the couch instead.

A feeling of accomplishment filled Colin, along with the strange sensation of belonging. Here. With Rina and her dog in this small Cape apartment. "Amazing," he said, unsure if he was referring to the tree or the feelings *she* inspired.

"I know. Even with remnants left in the stores, this tree looks just perfect." Her soft, grateful gaze met his and yearning flared to life between them.

He'd held off touching her all day, knowing the tree would never get put up or decorated if he even so much as stroked or kissed her soft skin. But the work was finished, and now the fun could begin. "We can't have sex by the fire on Christmas Eve, but there's no reason why we can't do it tonight."

She let out a husky purr of agreement and came into his arms. "But I thought we'd make New Year's resolutions first."

He blinked, surprised. "I'm not big on those." Mostly because they entailed promises, something he'd never been great at keeping. To distract her, he slipped his hands beneath her heavy wool sweater so his hands spanned her waist, traveling upward and coming to rest on the outside of her breasts. The full mounds filled his palms, warm, feminine flesh awaiting his touch.

"Force yourself. For me, okay? It's an old family

tradition, and I thought you and I could do it together this year."

Even if they wouldn't be together next year to reassess and reevaluate? Colin wondered silently. "You go first," he said instead.

"Okay." She scrunched her nose and she got lost, deep in thought. "I will continue to be true to myself."

"In what way?" he asked, intrigued.

"You know how some people undergo psychotherapy? Well, I don't have to. My column's been one huge lesson in self-awareness. And it's taught me a bigger lesson about you." She wrapped her hands around him, trapping his hands against her bare skin. "So, I'll continue to write my column and only let people and things that are good for me into my life."

"That's a tall order."

"I can handle it." She grinned and brushed a kiss over his lips. "Your turn."

He swallowed hard. "I'll be true to…" He wanted to say *you* but bit his tongue, knowing that kind of promise was impossible to keep. And any commitment he made to Rina, he intended to follow through upon.

"Come on, Colin. Don't take the easy way and just repeat what I said. Make a New Year's resolution," she urged.

"I resolve to take care of things in my life the most responsible way I can." Vague, but he hoped she wouldn't question him.

Because it was a holiday weekend, no one had returned his business calls, but he intended to start by having another talk with the accountants and seeing exactly what shape the paper was in now. His last figures had been from too far back. Then he needed to talk to Joe. Together, maybe they could come up with a plan that wouldn't hurt the people they both cared for, he thought, looking into Rina's wide-eyed gaze. But in the meantime, he couldn't deny that he'd been progressing with his plan, and he silently cursed Corinne for letting things slide so far that Colin had to put the pieces back together.

"See? That wasn't so difficult, was it?" she asked.

He forced a grin. "Of course not."

"And now we can pick up where we left off." Without warning, she reached down and pulled her sweater over her head until she stood before him in a pink lace bra, her pale skin lit by the flickering firelight.

He leaned forward, intending to kiss her, but she stopped him by pushing down on his shoulders, bringing him to his knees. She followed, eyeing him expectantly. The time for kissing had passed and he dipped his head. Starting at her navel, his tongue traced a pattern on her flat stomach and silken skin. He unhooked her bra and tossed it aside so he could encircle first one nipple with his mouth, then the next, tugging on the distended tip until her hips tilted forward and a strangled moan reverberated from her throat.

"Get undressed." Rina's demand sounded hoarse to her own ears.

She didn't care. She'd never felt such driving, overpowering need to be a part of another human being. To be one with Colin. Her hands shook as she reached for the button on his jeans, impatience overtaking her.

"Relax. We have all night."

Someone ought to tell that to her overheated body. He covered her hand, moving it away so he could take care of things himself. Quicker, she figured, than if she'd fumbled around.

Instead, she worked on her own clothes, meeting him naked on the floor. He pulled her on top of his warm, strong body, allowing her to feel his erection hot and ready against her stomach. She reached between them and a drop of his moisture touched her hand. A wash of desire and sensation swept through her, a heavy dampness filling the space between her legs.

Unable to wait, she straddled him, holding his hard length in one hand and him between her thighs. His gaze never left hers, hot and intense as she lowered herself, taking him in, inch by inch, feeling him swell and harden inside her. And just when she thought she couldn't take any more, she released the muscles in her legs and he filled her completely.

He reached out, grabbing her hands in his, intertwining their fingers. They couldn't be in a more intimate position. She sat up on his thighs, his penis embedded deep inside her, her entire upper body exposed for his view. When she glanced down, their joining was an erotic vision of two people becoming one. At the sight, her muscles contracted around him and his hips jerked upward, pressing on just the right place to increase the friction and orgasm-inducing sensation.

"Ride me, honey," Colin spoke through gritted teeth.

He shook from the effort of holding back, and Rina gave him what he asked for. Rising up, she felt every hard ridge ease out of her body before she came back down hard, bringing herself closer to the brink. He picked up on her rhythm. Bucking in and out, up and down, she lost herself in hot, sweaty, desire.

Without warning, the physical sensations swamping her mixed with raw emotion and Rina swallowed over a sob, one that came loud and ripped from inside her. God, she was close. He slipped his fingers between them, gliding over her clit, rolling his fingertips while they moved, bringing on an intense, explosive orgasm that seemed to go on and on and on.

AT RINA'S INSISTENCE, she and Colin spent Sunday morning with the rest of the crowds doing last-minute holiday shopping. They separated in the mall long enough for him to buy her a present before meeting up again later. Now, gifts under the tree, they were relaxing at her place when the doorbell rang.

She dropped the pad and paper. "They're here." She sprang from the chair where she'd been taking notes for her column and ran for the door.

Their solitude had officially ended, and Colin groaned. After making love in front of the fire, they'd showered, gone out for a quick burger, picked up a change of clothes for him, and returned to her place for the night. And what a night it had been. The woman had energy, stamina, and a completely giving nature, going so far as to insist Norton be allowed to join them when it came time for sleep. She didn't want the pooch to face another night alone.

Now the damn dog was his best friend. While Colin lay on the couch watching football, Norton sprawled on top of him, his face on Colin's stomach, his black tongue hanging out.

"What kind of dog doesn't jump when the door-bell rings?" he asked aloud.

"The dumbest kind," a male voice said from behind him.

Colin tried to rise but Norton wasn't budging.

"That's okay. If he's attached to you, he'll stay the hell away from me. I'm Jake. Rina's brother." The other man extended his hand and Colin shook it.

"Colin Lyons."

"Good to meet you. Rina's told me all about you."

That shocked him. He'd never thought about whether Rina discussed him with her family. If he had, he wouldn't have believed he was important enough for her to mention. It looked as though he'd have been wrong.

Jake studied Colin as if taking his measure. "Good game?" he asked, settling in on the couch, comfortable and at home.

Colin glanced at the television. "Not bad. How was your trip?"

Jake laughed. "Long, with too many pit stops."

In person, Colin could see the resemblance between the dark-haired cop and his sister.

A pretty auburn-haired woman came up around Jake, joining them, reminding Colin their private time had come to an end, at least for the weekend. But time with her family meant that he would be learning more about her, as he discovered over the next few hours. Her sister-in-law liked to talk, filling him in on Rina's life back in New York and how proud she and Jake were of her new job and column. She'd even mentioned how the glow in Rina's cheeks was more pronounced now with her new life underway, prompting an elbow in her arm from Rina.

Overall, Colin was overwhelmed by Rina's brother and sister-in-law. Her family's presence reminded him he hadn't visited Joe in the last day or so, and guilt compounded any fun he might have had. "Listen, since you have company, I'm going to head on over to the hospital to see Joe."

"His… father," Rina said by way of explanation.

"Hospital at Christmas? I'm sorry," Brianne said.

"Thanks."

Brianne smiled. "Do you plan to come back? I was hoping we'd have more time getting to know you this weekend."

"Colin?" Rina turned her gaze his way.

Knowing he couldn't deny her a thing even if it involved more family time, he nodded. "How about I go for a quick visit and come back after? That'll give you all some time alone." While he visited Joe in a hospital bed and Corinne in Dior's finest. He groaned, wishing not for the first time since Joe's remarriage that Nell was still alive and he had the family he'd grown up with instead of some awkward situation where Colin felt like a third wheel.

"Can you make it back by dinner?" Rina asked.

"You should try," Jake said. "Otherwise, you're leaving me alone with these two women and one wuss of a dog." He grinned, making his joke obvious before Rina could smack him.

"I'll see what I can do."

"That would be great. I really want the three of us to celebrate. Jake, did you read my columns?" Rina asked, shamelessly seeking praise.

Something Jake obviously realized because he laughed and pulled her into a brotherly embrace. "You know I'm proud of you, Ri."

So was Colin. Pride and admiration filled him, feelings at odds with promises already made. During halftime, he'd checked his cell to discover he'd missed a call from Ron Gold. The lender had wanted to know what progress Colin had made with Corinne, and he'd asked how soon the paper would begin its turnaround. Damn.

It was time he cornered Corinne again.

"I'll walk Colin out and be back in a few minutes." Rina followed him, stepping outside and shutting the door behind them. "I know you need to see Joe, but I hope you don't feel like we're pushing you out."

He cradled her cheek in his palm. "Of course not. It's just that being around your family reminded me I need to be more attentive to mine."

"You'll come back?" she asked.

She stepped closer, her body heat obvious despite the cold, attracting him, beckoning to him, offering him warmth that went beyond skin deep. "I'll come back," he promised.

Differences aside, he meant to keep his word.

COLIN PACED THE hallway. He couldn't bring himself to go back into Joe's room and watch Corinne fawn over his father, waving her perfumed wrist around and issuing orders to Colin to get more water and help her take care of Joe. He didn't need Corinne telling him what to do for the man he'd known most of his life.

He paused in the doorway of Joe's room, realizing the couple was having a hushed conversation. Joe was weak and hadn't done more than open his eyes. As a result of the stroke, he had slurred speech and Colin hadn't pressed him. But there he was with Corinne, her head bent, and soft whispers passing between them.

As he'd come to believe by watching Corinne over the last week, there was more to this relationship than he'd originally believed. Hell, there'd have to be more to Joe and Corinne's marriage than sex or convenience or even money for Joe to give her power of attorney and control of the paper instead of giving that control to *his son*.

Logan had been right all along. The adoption papers called Colin Joe's son, but more and more, Colin was coming to feel shut out. Belonging nowhere and to no one. A tight knot constricted his chest, making breathing difficult. He wished he could blame the antiseptic hospital smells, but something else was at work and Colin didn't like it worth a damn.

He also didn't like the waiting. Unfortunately, the time of year and the circumstances with Joe left him without a choice. There'd be no talking to Corinne now.

Colin slipped back into the hall, nearly colliding with a nurse and her lunch cart on the way out. "Sorry," he muttered.

Making his way to the elevators, he only wanted to get the hell out of here.

Away from the family he didn't really have, the place he didn't belong. He needed to be with Rina. She made him feel accepted, whole in a way he'd never been. But the last thing he wanted to deal with was another family situation where he was the outsider.

He'd promised her he'd come back, but he wasn't ready now. In fact, he was one step away from jumping on a plane and saying to hell with them all. His love for Joe wouldn't allow it, of course, not until things with the paper were settled.

But the stronger pull came not from his father fig-ure, but from Rina, or more accurately, the feelings she inspired in him. Feelings that were growing beyond anything he'd anticipated or knew how to deal with.

SINCE BRIANNE AND Jake insisted they wanted to spend the night in a hotel and not put her out, Rina had the evening to herself. Of course, she wouldn't be alone if Colin had shown up as he'd promised. But she was coming to realize Colin didn't keep promises. He didn't know how, she thought sadly.

In her heart, she knew he hadn't meant to hurt her, not when he'd left her at Emma's party and not tonight. Ironically, writing about what men wanted was helping her sort out her relationship with Colin. Once she'd gotten past sex appeal, attraction, and attitude, she had to ask herself what kept people together. And what immediately came to mind was understanding, something Colin needed.

Anger would only drive him away. Rina suspected losing his parents had left him unable to deal with his feelings, and so, when things got out of control, he withdrew. As he had when his parents died, and as he had when his marriage went bad. Even Rina had seen him run more than once. Being around her family hadn't been easy for him. She'd seen his clenched jaw and occasional restless pacing. Until he faced his past and his feelings, understanding was the only thing she could offer him now.

Unable to help herself or Colin, she decided to share her insight with her readers and sat down in front of the computer. With the upcoming new year, Rina hoped that more relationships would be strengthened than lost. That was the point of her column, after all. Too bad she, personally, couldn't count on that optimistic outcome.

By the time she typed the last sentence and glanced up, over two hours had passed. She saved her document, then emailed to Corinne. Cathartic as well as productive, this week's column, entitled "Of One Mind: Getting Inside Your Man's Head," was ready.

She'd gone way beyond the first article that detailed superficial things like hair and makeup. Once a woman landed a man, those frills still counted but the heart and soul had something at stake, too.

She stood and stretched her cramped muscles, feeling proud of a job well done. Except for Colin's absence, life was very good right now and would be even better once she soaked in a nice, warm, strawberry-scented bath. She pulled her hair on top of her head, changed into a robe, ran the water, and was just about to climb into the tub when the doorbell rang. Norton jumped up from the bathroom floor and ran for the front door.

Rina followed, assuming Frankie had come by to tell her about the date she'd accepted with a coworker. One thing Rina could say for her friend, she didn't have a problem getting an initial date. Apparently, Rina's bath would have to wait.

Commiserating about men couldn't. But when she opened the door, instead of Frankie, she found a surprise visitor leaning against the door frame. "Colin!"

"Hi," he said, then wedged his foot in the doorway.

Obviously, he assumed she'd slam the door in his face. He couldn't be more wrong.

She inhaled his masculine scent and memories of having him inside her body ricocheted through her. "Come on in." She figured that was a start.

After shutting the door behind him, she turned to meet his gaze.

"Don't hate me, Rina. I couldn't handle that." He laid a hand on her shoulder and his fingertips brushed the sensitive skin on her neck.

She shivered, his touch more sensual than apologetic. "I didn't expect to see you again tonight. Or any other time this weekend, to be honest."

Because her family would still be around, Rina had counted Colin out. The fact that he was here now gave her a ridiculous amount of hope for a woman who'd just admitted to herself that she accepted this man for the wanderer he was.

Exhaustion strained his expression, and her heart went out to him. He ran a hand through his hair. "When I left the hospital, at first I needed to be alone. To get away from everyone and everything."

His fingers tangled in the stray strands of her hair, causing her pulse to hammer wildly and her mouth to grow dry.

He led her inside and together they sat on the couch. Rina curled her legs beneath her.

"I wasn't ready to deal with another family situation."

He'd confirmed her hunch. One part of her liked knowing she understood him so well, another part was disappointed that he'd fallen back into old patterns.

"Especially another one where I was an outsider." He held out his hand and waited.

He obviously wanted her understanding. She'd already promised herself she'd provide it, and now she knew why. *She loved him.* Flaws and all, *she loved* this man who found himself unable to handle emotion or commitment.

Seconds passed, in which the roar in her ears and the silent echo of the words were the only sounds she heard. *She loved him.* Because of Colin, she'd come to understand her past and her marriage, and she knew not only what she wanted, but what she deserved out of life. Colin would never demand self-sacrifice.

He'd never ask her to give up the career she loved or the life she'd created. He might leave in the end, but he'd given her something precious to keep in her heart. He'd given her his understanding. In return, because she loved and accepted him, she'd reciprocate by letting him go.

She placed her palm inside his. The sizzling sexual tension sprang to life once more. Only this time she knew more than desire crackled between them. Because the heart she thought she'd protected belonged to him.

Chapter Ten

"WHAT HAPPENED AT the hospital?" Rina asked.

Colin shrugged. He leaned back into the cushioned sofa and glanced up at the ceiling, his pain obvious. "Watching Corinne at Joe's bedside made me... uncomfortable."

"Why?" She needed details if she was going to help him through this. That he'd come to her now showed how much faith he placed in them. She didn't want to let him down.

"All this time, I've been blaming her for working her wiles on Joe and destroying the family we used to have."

"And now?" Rina asked, leading but wanting him to confide on his own.

"I accepted something I probably knew all along but wasn't ready to face."

Rina squeezed his hand tighter. "Which is?"

"Corinne's not the outsider, I am."

She had a family she'd never feel left out of. Colin didn't, and his words hit Rina hard, helping her to understand him even more. Still, maybe his vision was distorted, coming from the perspective of the little boy who'd lost his parents and then felt as if he'd had no one.

"I know that's your perception and I've never met Joe, but my heart tells me he wouldn't agree. The man took you into his home. He adopted you. That says something about his feelings for you. Did you talk to him today?"

"I didn't want to be in a place I didn't belong, so I took off."

"So, what brought you back here now?"

He rolled his head to the side, meeting her gaze. "You're the only one I trust enough to let in." He pointed to his chest. "Here." He tapped the area over his heart.

A lump rose to her throat as he reached out and touched her cheek.

"Am I forgiven?"

"There never was anything to forgive."

He released a long breath, and she felt as if she'd given him a gift.

Still, she sensed he wasn't finished, that he had more to reveal. "What else did you realize today?" she asked.

"Are you a mind reader?" he asked, laughing.

"No, but I guess I am coming to know you."

Gratitude flickered in his gaze. "Joe raised me as

his son. From plain old discipline to learning journalism at his knee, he didn't treat me any differently than if he'd had a kid of his own."

"That says so much about his character. He's obviously a good man."

"I know. That's what makes this so hard to reconcile. When Joe got sick, who did he give power of attorney? Who did he trust with his biggest, most beloved asset? With the asset he taught *me* to love and respect? Not his *son,* but his wife of two years."

She heard the betrayal in Colin's voice. She felt his pain in her heart. Her words wouldn't offer any explanation or ease his hurt, but she instinctively knew exactly what he needed. Something she could provide.

Turning toward him, she held out her arms, waiting as he came forward, his lips sealing hard and fast against hers.

Rina's lips devoured Colin's with abandon, not holding back. His blood heated and blazed, desire threatening to rampage out of control.

"Let's take this into the bedroom," he suggested, breaking the kiss.

He had no doubt she'd agree. Her body spoke for her, telling him she wanted him as much as he wanted her. But more importantly, she'd listened and understood, offering the comfort he needed without him having to ask.

"Sounds like a good plan," she said, her brown eyes glittering bright with desire.

Rising from the couch, he picked her up and swept her into his arms. "You should know I didn't come back here expecting this."

She laughed and shook her head before running a finger down his cheek. "Liar."

Caught, he merely grinned. "Okay, let's say I needed you and leave it at that."

"That's more like the silver-tongued devil you usually are."

He laughed. Her acceptance filled an emptiness inside him. He could have said that gnawing hole had begun with Joe's illness, but the empty pit had been eating away at him for a long time. Since his parents' deaths.

And that emptiness had led to the need to fill the void. He'd fallen back on travel, and the old desire was beckoning again. But he hadn't been able to outrun the void in the past and he knew it wouldn't accomplish anything now. He was fighting it this time, but it was difficult.

The woman in his arms made it easier. He made his way to the bedroom with her nuzzling at his neck, her breath warm against his skin. Without warning, she began to tug at his earlobe with her teeth. The sensation was hot and erotic, shooting desire straight to his cock. She'd not only chased away the pain but *she'd* filled the emptiness.

The realization struck him hard, but before he could deal with what that meant, he'd reached the bed and more urgent needs called to him.

He lowered her to the comforter and came down on top of her in the nick of time, spreading her thighs and settling his hard, aching erection between her legs. Though he was fully dressed, he realized she wasn't.

Her robe parted easily, and instead of thin silk, he discovered bare flesh, heat, and her needy sex waiting for his touch and his taste. He curled his fingers around the down comforter surrounding them and prayed for restraint.

"Don't you think you're overdressed?" she asked.

To hell with it. Restraint was overrated. He rose and began stripping out of his clothes, mindless of where they fell but not unaware of Rina. She watched him undress. Her bright gaze followed his movements, the need dilating her eyes an arousing sight. As was her pose. She lay on the bed, robe parted, exposing a hint of white skin and cleavage above the belted knot.

He eased himself beside her, fully naked and completely aroused. Flesh against flesh, he thought he'd died and gone to heaven except for the hard ache he'd yet to satisfy.

"I have a surprise." Her light laughter only served

to inflame his need even more.

"I like surprises."

"Then close your eyes."

He lay back and complied, his body charged, his mind barely able to focus. In the darkness, he heard her open a drawer and rummage through it. "No peeking," she warned him.

He covered his eyes with one arm for good measure.

"Ready?" she asked in a husky voice.

"That's a loaded question, Rina." And then he nearly flew off the bed as he felt the first silken touch of... "What is that?"

"What's it feel like?"

"A soft tingling," he said through gritted teeth as a featherlight sensation teased his skin and worked its way up his thighs. "A feather?"

"Wrong."

The fluttering torment continued as she caressed his lower abdomen, flirting with him, circling close to where his erection pulsed thick and ready.

"Guess again."

The sensation came once more, this time teasing the head of his cock, causing his hips to jerk upward. He nearly came then. Unable and unwilling to play anymore, he opened his eyes.

Rina straddled his thighs, a long ponytail in her

hand, a warm, inviting smile on her flushed face. "I remember how much you liked the long hair, so I thought I'd satisfy that ultimate male fantasy."

"What male fantasy?"

"Wrapping long hair around your body. Don't tell me it's not something you've dreamed about." She studied him through too-innocent eyes for a woman so bewitching.

"If I admit to the obvious, do you think we can do something about this?" He glanced at his unrestrained erection.

"I think that can be arranged." With a wicked grin, she tossed the hair extension aside and covered his thighs with splayed hands, inching upward until her fingertips touched his coarse hair.

He let out a groan. This woman would be the death of him.

"But first, I need you to tell me what you want." She swallowed hard and hesitated, the uncertainty more endearing than her earlier boldness had been.

He'd once asked her to tell him the same thing, and he was grateful she'd cared enough to ask. "I want you to take me in your mouth." He needed her to give to him that way. Needed to know she was as far gone as he. "Grip me in your hand, take me in your mouth, and make me come."

He held his breath and waited as she stretched out

beside him, her legs near his head, her mouth hovering above his sex. "A first," he thought he heard her say, and then he heard nothing because she'd done as he'd asked.

Heat enveloped him, cushioning him in liquid warmth. At the first lap of her tongue, he nearly came off the bed. And then she bathed him with long sweeps of her tongue, alternating with erotic grazing of teeth against his cock.

"Sweet heaven," he muttered with an uncontrollable groan. He was lost in the most incredible whirlpool of sensation but not so far gone he couldn't think of her, and when he opened his eyes, her bare skin beckoned to him.

It took some maneuvering and some concentration on his part not to come first, but he managed to part her robe and find the vee of her legs. He grasped her thighs and placed his mouth on her feminine heat, finding her wet and wanting.

"Colin?"

The shock in her voice sounded at the same time the swirling arousing sensations rocking his body tapered off. Damn. "Relax, sweetheart. I want you with me when I come."

The things Rina did to him, body, heart, and soul defied description. He inhaled her scent and his body trembled as he began working her again with his tongue.

A whimper escaped, bubbling up from the back of her throat, and her hips began a subtle gyration, begging for more. Holding on to her thighs, he met her silent demand as she did the same for him, slickening his hard shaft with her mouth and gliding her hands up and down, mimicking the thrust of his body pumping into her tight heat.

Within seconds, a shaking, shuddering climax hit him, harder than any he could remember, sending him into a breath-stealing moment of release and complete surrender. From the cry that escaped her lips, he knew he'd taken her along for the ride. And that notion pleased him far more than his own physical release.

LATER, AFTER A shower that involved more than washing up, they shared popcorn in bed music from her phone played in the background. A dim light set the room aglow, Rina snuggled beside him, and Colin felt a contentment that had always eluded him.

"I've been thinking," she said.

"I know. I can hear those old gears grinding."

She laughed. "I'm serious. You were talking earlier about how hurt you were that Joe didn't leave the running of the paper to you in case of an emergency."

The topic sobered him, reminding him of how and

why he'd ended up back on Rina's doorstep tonight. Watching Corinne sit by Joe's bedside, her gaze wet, his hand in hers, he'd felt like an outsider in a family he thought had been his. He wasn't a child and he understood how juvenile his thoughts seemed, so he'd tried to focus on the reasons behind his feelings.

It came back to the bond he'd always shared with Joe. The bond the older man had broken. The newspaper. "What about it?" he asked Rina.

"Well, I take it that Joe hasn't been up to a business conversation for awhile now, so you don't know why he did what he did."

"That about sums it up."

"Until you can talk with him, you won't feel much better. But you can try talking to Corinne and not fighting with her," she suggested. "I did notice you aren't exactly your charming self when she's around."

Despite the serious subject, he laughed. "That's true." He picked up a piece of popcorn. "Open," he said. Rina opened her mouth, and he popped a piece inside. "But I have tried, and she's set on doing things her way. And I went there today, intending to hash things out, but..." He shook his head. "It wasn't the time."

She chewed and swallowed. "Well, you're the one with experience," she said, taking his side without knowing what his side was or what it would mean for her future. "As soon as Joe's better, I'm sure he'll hear you out."

"The doctor's indicated a return to work wasn't coming anytime soon," he said.

"But he'll be able to take back the reins or at least oversee more. At the very least, you'll be able to talk to him again." She leaned over and placed a salty kiss on his lips. "You'll feel better once you get things off your chest. Be true to yourself, Colin. I already told you, my marriage taught me that's the one thing that counts in life."

"You told me a little. I want to know more."

She eyed him steadily. "I realize now that though I did love Robert…" She trailed off.

And he hated the jealousy gnawing at his gut. Hating the thought of Rina with any other man.

"Although I loved him, it was a steady, dependable kind of love." She drew a calming breath. "Not anything like…" She shook her head, interrupting herself. "Never mind."

Colin's stomach clenched, but he refused to push her. Probably because he was afraid she'd compare her safe marriage to their more-combustible, less-reliable, short-term affair. And he wasn't in any position to reassure her.

✧　✧　✧

RINA DECIDED TO throw a last-minute party on Christmas Day. Instead of having Colin uncomfortable and surrounded only by her family, she wanted to bring his friends and relatives to him.

Luckily, Logan and Catherine agreed to move their holiday celebration to Rina's, and Catherine even offered to bring the food, for which Rina was eternally grateful. Catherine then talked her sister, Kayla, and her husband, Kane, into joining them. Frankie had also agreed since her family was out of state and she hadn't made any plans. And Emma had jumped with glee, accepting any excuse to spend Christmas with Logan and away from her son. She'd even asked if she could bring Stan.

Progress came in many forms, Rina thought wryly as her company all mingled in the family room. Rina's only concern was whether Norton would behave. She glanced down at the offending male, who stared up at her with soulful eyes.

He didn't like having his home invaded by so many people who ignored him or refused to pass him food. "You will be good, won't you, boy?"

"If you insist on wearing that dress, I can't promise a thing."

Rina turned. Colin stood in the doorway, staring at her hungrily from across the expanse of the small kitchen. "For a minute there, I thought Norton was answering me."

He laughed, stepping toward her. "You look incredible."

Heat flooded her cheeks, but she was glad he'd noticed. "You're not so bad yourself."

"Now, there's a compliment," he said wryly. "Are you really worried about Norton? I can walk him if you are."

She shrugged. "I'm just being cautious. He's not too happy with so many people in his space. Except for you. He adores you. And so do I." She brushed a kiss on his clean-shaven cheek, inhaling his seductive, purely masculine scent. Delicious, she thought.

She couldn't get enough of him. No matter how dangerous the thought, she had no choice but to accept what he gave and put the notion of him moving on out of her mind. It would happen soon enough, especially if things with Joe didn't go well.

Forcing herself to think about the party and the guests instead of making love with Colin wasn't easy. "You can walk him in about an hour. Right now, he's just sulking."

Colin cocked his head to the side, taking in the morose dog. "How can you tell?"

"Because he's not jumping and begging for attention. He wants these people to come to him. He went through a period like this after his stint as a hero dog.

He saved Brianne from a drug dealer who wanted revenge on my brother. He got so spoiled afterward it took a while until he started acting like a normal canine again."

Colin raised an eyebrow in surprise. "I didn't think he had a vicious bone in his wrinkled body."

She laughed. "He doesn't. He didn't even have to bare his teeth. All he had to do was pee on the guy's leg. The bad guy lost his focus, giving Jake a chance to step in."

Colin grinned. "Way to use your bodily functions, man."

Norton thumped his tail in reply.

"Hey, I thought I was the hero who rescued Brianne." Jake entered the kitchen.

"Only after Norton provided the opportunity, and don't you forget it. You owe him."

"I paid in advance by watching him that entire summer," he muttered.

"I'm sure it wasn't that much of a hardship." She folded her arms over her chest. "And I didn't realize you were standing there."

He folded his arms over his chest, too, a gesture very much like Rina's, Colin thought.

"I'm just observing," Jake said, his gaze on Colin.

Observing him, Colin realized. Rina hadn't said anything, but it was obvious his decision not to return yesterday had impacted not just Rina but her brother. Jake's attitude had been decidedly chillier than yesterday. Colin respected that.

"So, what can I get you guys? Colin?" she asked first, obviously attempting to change the subject.

"Do you have any bottled water? Emma's getting tipsy and Logan wants to dilute her wine."

Rina furrowed her eyebrows. "Emma doesn't drink. She's up to something, so you'd better keep an eye on her. Better yet, keep an eye on poor Stan. The man has his hands full." She turned to her brother. "And you? Isn't your wife waiting inside?"

"As a matter of fact, she wants to know if you have any celery."

Rina crinkled her nose. "Cat's hot appetizers are so good. Why would Brianne want celery?"

Jake rolled his eyes skyward. "As if I have a clue what women think."

"Hmm. That might be a good subject for my next series of articles. How to get inside a woman's head." She grinned. "I like that."

"Works for me," Jake muttered.

Colin swallowed hard and remained silent.

"Brianne also wants peanut butter," Jake said. "And some raisins if you have them. Oh, and she'd like a large glass of milk."

Colin grimaced. "That's what I call disgusting."

"It's what I'd call a craving," Rina said, her eyes opening wide.

"What?" Jake walked over to Rina, obviously picking up on her choice of words. "What are you talking about?"

"Brianne's got odd cravings. Could there be any special reason for them?" Rina wiggled her eyebrows knowingly while Jake, the macho cop, suddenly looked green.

"To hell with the celery," he said and bolted for the other room to talk to his wife.

Rina laughed. "Mission accomplished. Jake's out of here and we can squeeze in a minute alone."

"You went to all this trouble, arranged this party, all for me. Do you know how lucky I am to have you?" He wrapped his arms around her waist and pulled her to him. She smelled like Rina, an arousing floral scent that seeped into his bones. He smelled it in his sleep.

"Mmm. As long as you know how lucky you are, that's all that counts." She linked her hands around his neck and pulled him into a hot, tongue-tangling kiss.

But before things could get any deeper, a ringing cell phone interrupted them. With a groan, Colin reached for his phone while Rina stepped back, resigned.

"Hello?"

"Merry Christmas, Colin." He recognized Corinne's voice.

His heart clenched in fear. "Same to you. Is Joe okay?" he asked, knowing she wouldn't call without good reason.

"Actually, he's doing well today. Holiday spirits and all that. He'd like to see you."

Fear turned to anticipation. "I'd planned on coming to the hospital after dinner."

"Could you make it before then? Actually, can you make it now? Joe's strength is up and it's a good time for the two of you to talk."

"Go," Rina whispered, obviously having overheard. "I understand."

He didn't want to leave, if only because he didn't want to walk out on her again. But he needed to see Joe and he couldn't let the opportunity slip by. "Tell him I'll be there," he said to Corinne.

"Thanks."

Colin hung up and slipped the phone into his pocket, shooting Rina a regret-filled look. "I wish—"

"Shh." She put a finger to his lips. "It's Christmas. You should be with Joe. I'd go with you, but I have a houseful of people."

He placed his hand beneath her chin, tilting her face up toward him. "You thought about going with me. That means a lot."

He bent to kiss her and, as usual, the kiss flared out of control. She teased him with her tongue, tracing the seam of his lips and darting inside before she pulled away.

"Just wanted to give you a taste. Come back tonight and I'll give you even more." A wicked gleam flickered in her gaze, making him laugh. He'd already grown hard with wanting her.

Getting through the day, his desire unrelieved, would be hell. Dealing with Joe and the subject of family, the paper, and Corinne would be even worse.

"Hey, you two, quit necking and get inside for a toast," Emma said, banging on the wall by the kitchen, making her presence known. "It's rude to make out when you have company waiting. I, on the other hand, do not have company. So, would you mind pointing out the least trafficked area so I can get my dear Stan alone?"

Colin rolled his eyes.

Rina laughed. "Probably the bathroom since this is a small place. Sorry, Emma, but today won't be the most romantic day you'll ever spend."

She wagged her wrinkled finger at Rina. "That's where you're wrong. It's the person you are with, not your surroundings that matters. Now, get inside. Your brother wants to make a toast."

And then he'd head over to the hospital, Colin

thought, uncertain of whether to dread or look forward to the meeting. As they stepped inside, Jake tapped a knife against a glass and the talking dwindled. "I'd just like to say a few words. First, I don't know most of you, but thanks for taking care of my sister since she's moved here."

Colin squeezed Rina's hand tight.

"Second, I want to toast her determination to make a new life and her success in going after what she's always wanted. My sister is now a columnist and happier than I've ever seen her. Here's to health and happiness, Ri."

Rina blushed, an adorable shade of pink. But with every one of Jake's words, Colin's gut twisted tighter. Because he knew he was heading over to the hospital to finally discuss the paper's financial situation and future with Joe. A future that might not include Rina.

She wanted to continue her column and live life on her own terms the way her ex-husband had never allowed her to do. Could Colin destroy her dreams just so he could achieve his own goals? January 1 was around the corner, and even if Colin managed an extension, it would only delay the inevitable. Unless he came up with another solution or performed magic. Neither seemed likely.

"And lastly," Jake said, bringing Colin back to the other man's toast, "I want to let all of you in on the fact that my beautiful wife and I are officially expecting a baby, something I just discovered myself. So, cheers, everyone, and Merry Christmas." He raised his glass and everyone toasted, clicking glasses and murmuring good wishes.

Colin glanced at Rina's wide smile. "You don't seem surprised by this news. You weren't fishing when you sent your brother out of the room earlier?"

She shrugged, looking like the proverbial cat who ate the canary. "I had a *very* strong hunch. I'm just glad to be right. I'm going to be an aunt!" Her voice rose in excitement as she glanced back at her brother and Brianne.

"You like kids, huh?" Now, where the hell had *that* come from?

"Is this a trick question?" She met his gaze, a wry smile on her lips. "I say no, you think I'm a witch? I say yes, you run for cover before I can con you into having one? It *is* every single man's worst fear realized, right?"

He brushed his knuckles over her cheek. "Until he meets the right woman." And then, before things could get too serious, he said, "I have to get going."

She nodded. "I know talking to Joe won't be easy, but you need to do what I said. You need to be true to yourself."

His heart constricted at her serious words and earnest gaze. She cared so much and gave even more. But she had no idea just what her advice would cost her.

Chapter Eleven

R INA LOVED THE holidays. The music, the festive cheer, the people surrounding her. She just wished she'd been able to help Colin more, but maybe meeting with Joe would do the trick.

Emma tapped her foot impatiently against the floor and Rina realized she was being chastised. She also knew what for. "What would you like me to do?" she asked, meeting the older woman's annoyed gaze. "I can't just take off after Colin."

Much as she'd like to. She didn't want him to be alone when dealing with Joe in case the older man's explanation provided more hurt than solution.

"Why can't you leave? It's not like someone here can't hold down the fort while you're gone." Emma shot her a pointed glare.

"You of all people understand etiquette. I can't walk out on my own party. It's rude."

"I beg to differ. Catherine's a caterer and she'd be happy to keep the hors d'oeuvres hot until you get back. Wouldn't you?" Emma grasped Catherine's sleeve as she walked by.

"Wouldn't I what?" the pretty blonde asked.

"Hold down the food, I mean fort, while Rina goes to the hospital to be by Colin's side."

"Of course." Cat waved a hand in dismissal. "You go on and don't worry about a thing here."

"But…"

"And while Catherine handles the food, Francesca doesn't mind serving as hostess, do you, dear?" The older woman had to hustle, but she managed to poke Frankie in the back as she passed. "I'd play hostess myself but I'm being paged," Emma said.

To Rina's shock, Emma turned and blew a kiss Stan's way.

"I'll be right there," she called to the man who sat in the corner, patting the arm of the chair as if he wanted Emma to join him.

Frankie chuckled. "I can handle things here," she assured Emma and Rina.

Rina glanced around. She had to admit, she could probably sneak off for an hour and they'd survive.

But Colin was facing an emotional minefield. Would he welcome her presence? Or would showing up give him a reason to push her away?

HALF AN HOUR later, Rina walked into the hospital, and after meeting up with Corinne on Joe's floor, was directed to his room. She strode into the doorway and paused. Colin sat in the chair beside the bed, his back to the door and his head bent close to the man he called his father.

The intensity in the room was fierce and a lump rose to her throat. Her pulse began to pound and her heart raced, anticipation and anxiety feuding inside her. She didn't know what Colin was facing. But as much as she wanted to go to him, to hold his hand, she remained in the shadows, knowing he deserved his time alone.

Knowing, too, she'd be here when it was through.

CORINNE HAD LEFT Colin alone with Joe, destroying any lingering notions Colin might have had about her exerting undue influence on Joe. Not that he had many left anyway. After a solid week of watching her at Joe's bedside, he was convinced of her sincerity, not that it was an easy thing to admit.

"Did you ever have a dream?" Joe asked.

"Of course, I've dreamed." Colin forced a laugh as the older man stared without speaking, an old tactic he'd used on Colin as a teenager. One that to this day never failed to elicit a response. "I've dreamed of running the paper."

"Bullshit" Joe spoke loud, clear, and less slurred than before. The effort obviously cost him because he leaned back against the white pillow. "You don't know your dreams, and until you stop running, you never will."

A punch in the stomach would have been more gentle, but then, gentle had never been Joe's style. Directness had, which was why Corinne's power of attorney had taken Colin off guard. Joe hadn't prepared him up front.

Seconds passed in which Joe just met Colin's gaze and stared, while Colin tried to formulate a response when he had none. Because, as usual, the older man was right.

Joe gestured to the water pitcher. Grateful for a minute to think, Colin poured the cold liquid into a disposable cup, waiting for Joe to take a few sips before taking the cup back and placing it on the tray.

"If I'd have asked you to run the paper when I got sick, months before I had the stroke, I'd have been forcing you to come home for who knows how long. And you needed to find your way without my influence." He cleared his throat. "I've always considered you a son. Even when you couldn't return the sentiment."

Colin swallowed hard. "I returned it. I just couldn't show it. I thought I'd be betraying my parents."

Hard as Joe and Nell tried, Colin realized now they'd never completely filled the parental role, probably because he'd been old enough to maintain love and loyalty. And fear. Fear if he gave himself over to Joe and Nell's love, he'd lose his parents for good. Never mind that he'd already lost them.

Joe's laugh sounded more like a rasping wheeze, scaring Colin. "I knew that. Hell, Nell knew it, too. We never held it against you, though. That sense of loyalty was what made you such a damn fine man, one I'm proud to call my son."

Colin shook his head. "I never deserved you."

"You damn well did. You still do. You think I don't know you're here now, fighting to save what's mine? Only a son would do that for his father."

Colin closed his eyes but he couldn't shut out the truth. Joe knew him better than he knew himself. The older man understood things about Colin he himself had just come to recognize and accept. The running, the emotional barriers, all a result of his parents' deaths, had distanced him from his life and the people in it. But no longer.

It had taken Joe's stroke to bring him home, Joe's seeming betrayal to shock him into looking deeper, but it had been Rina who'd taught him the biggest lesson of all in understanding, acceptance—and love.

He shook as the word ran through his mind and settled there. He loved Rina. Something he'd deal with when he left the hospital.

And he loved the older man lying in the bed before him. "I'm lucky to have you. Always have been," Colin told Joe. "But why didn't you just tell me about giving Corinne power of attorney?"

Joe's brown eyes clouded over. "When I got sick, no way did I want to call you home, so when the doctors insisted I cut back, I put Corinne in charge."

"She knows nothing about running a paper, Joe."

"But I love and trust her, just like I do you. Just like I did Nell before her." He gestured for the water and Colin passed the cup again, waiting while Joe finished soothing his dry throat.

Hearing how Joe felt about his wife made Colin's mission to enlighten his father about the paper's problems more difficult. Colin ran a hand over his eyes and groaned.

He didn't know how to approach the issue and since he still didn't have a direct answer to his question, he focused on that first. "Then why didn't you *tell* me you put Corinne in charge?" he asked again.

"Because it wasn't something I felt I could do long distance. I knew you'd come home for Christmas, even if it was a short visit. I planned to tell you then. But fate intervened, and I had the damn stroke first." Joe's voice returned to a low whisper he had to strain to hear, but there was no mistaking the regret in his voice.

The vise holding Colin's heart hostage eased with the realization that everything Joe did had been in Colin's best interest. At the expense of his beloved paper.

Be true to yourself, Rina had said. The time had come. For father and son to work out a solution together. He rose from his seat and began pacing the floor, his gaze never leaving Joe's bed. "The *Times* has limited space, and Corinne's been sacrificing hard news for softer pieces." He no longer considered Rina's dreams fluff. Not since seeing how important they were to her and the reaction of people he admired, like Logan and Cat. "We're not putting out true news on the front or home page. Corinne's hired a woman named Rina Lowell to write about relationships, while Emma's doing a matchmaking column for the elderly. Our numbers and advertising have suffered," he said, forcing the words out.

He hated to hurt Joe, and he realized he hated to hurt Corinne, the woman he now understood Joe loved. But the older man didn't blink at the information.

Colin narrowed his gaze. "You knew this was coming, didn't you?"

He nodded. "I wasn't feeling well even before the stroke, and she didn't want to tell me she was having problems. But she finally told me she'd made some mistakes."

An understatement if Colin ever heard one.

"But," Joe continued. "She was determined to fix things and make me proud."

"You don't sound angry."

He shrugged. "When you face death, you realize there are more important things in life than selling newspapers."

Colin scrubbed a hand over his burning eyes. "Well, I'm about to complicate things." He explained how they'd lost advertising dollars and were poised to lose more. And then he topped off his story with the fact that he'd borrowed money to keep the paper afloat. "And like me, Ron thought you'd want nothing more than to have things return to the status quo. I promised him I'd get rid of the fluff in favor of hard news, and according to Fortune, I have until January first to provide proof I can do that or they're pulling out."

"And how exactly did you plan to save the paper from my terrible clutches, Colin?" Corinne walked into the room at the worst possible moment.

"By getting your promise to return things to the way they were." He didn't turn to face her, but he had to admit the truth. "And by getting rid of your new columnists." That had always been the plan, replace the new people's work with news worth printing. Only now, discussing his plans aloud, he realized how shortsighted he'd been.

"You wanted to fire Rina and Emma?" Corinne asked, outraged.

He winced, knowing he no longer advocated that scenario, but nodded because that had been his intention. But he now realized that, like Joe said, some things *were* more important. His family, Corinne included, was one of them. Rina another.

It was time to face Corinne and explain his change of heart. He turned, but behind Corinne, he saw Rina in the doorway and his stomach plummeted.

Eyes wide and full of hurt, she met his gaze. His gut clenched hard. Damn. "Rina."

She turned, pivoting and walking away. He stepped toward the door, then paused, looking back at the man in the bed.

"Don't you think you should go after her?" Corinne asked.

Colin was torn, but with Joe so ill, he had to take opportunity when he could and mend fences here first. "I'll talk to her as soon as we finish." Facing Corinne wasn't easy. "My perspective has changed even if the promise I made hasn't. And I'd like to explain."

Corinne nodded. "Seems fair."

"Then both of you sit," Joe said. "It's time we started acting like a family."

Although his heart was with Rina, Colin did as Joe asked. They talked like a family for the first time. When it was over, Colin knew they had a chance of saving the paper. Corinne agreed not to touch the remainder of the lender's money on anything without Colin's approval. With Joe supporting her columns, she was more agreeable to putting the news on the front and home pages.

In return, Colin was willing to invest the rest of the lender's money in creating a supplement section that would carry her beloved columns as well as the syndicated ones Colin had already lined up to return.

All that remained was working the magic he'd thought of earlier. He had to prove to the conservative Fortune's Inc. that Rina, Emma, and Corinne's other ideas would increase sales if they weren't the sole focus of the paper. Ironically, he'd use Corinne's argument that people's priorities had changed, and they could sell newspapers by combining news and softer pieces. If a simple phone call wouldn't do it, Colin would resort to statistical proof, something that would cost money and take time. He hoped he could at least get a deadline extension out of Fortune's.

By the time he left the hospital, Colin felt more centered about his family situation, but he still had to settle things with Rina. After not returning yesterday, Colin wasn't about to repeat the same mistake and compound her anger over what she'd overheard.

Instead, he showed up in time to suffer through a frosty Christmas dinner. And he wasn't referring to the weather outside. Rina barely spoke to him and he couldn't say he blamed her. He also couldn't find time to talk to her alone, and since Jake and Brianne planned to stay late, he had no choice but to wait until work in the morning. And he wasn't surprised when Rina didn't walk him to the door to say good night.

He let himself out, disappointment in his gut and her Christmas gift still in his pocket.

MONDAY MORNING, RINA called in sick. She wasn't ill. She was merely informed and armed with knowledge. She intended to protect herself and her future. She had no choice since she was about to lose the job she loved. True, eavesdroppers didn't always hear correctly, but Corinne had been by her side, peppering Colin with questions, and his words had left no doubt. He intended to *get rid of Corinne's columnists.* Herself and Emma.

Which meant that from the day he'd turned that incredible charm her way, he'd *known* he had an agenda. Her series of articles and research had taught her to understand and not jump to irrational conclusions. She could understand Colin's desperate need to save the paper from financial ruin, something else she'd been in the dark about. And when they'd first met and he didn't know her, she couldn't blame him for having an agenda that would negatively impact her.

But she couldn't understand the lingering deception. That was the hardest thing to grasp, Rina thought, and an even more difficult thing to forgive.

How could he have listened to her hopes and dreams, all the while knowing he intended to crush them, and never reveal a thing? How could he have made love to her and not tell her something so fundamentally important? And worst of all, how could he hear her revelations about her marriage, discover she'd come through one relationship where she'd lost sight of herself and her dreams, and not reveal his plans to take away hers?

Well, she thought, silence could go both ways. She'd gone out of her way to be understanding of his past, his need for emotional distance, and the fact that his desire to travel would take him away one day. But his behavior toward her was a direct slap, and Rina didn't feel the need to roll over and take it lying down.

Ironically, Colin himself had provided her with her new plan, and she had taken today off to update her résumé and e-mail her job queries to magazine editors in New York. Now, all she needed to do was wait for replies. As much as she loved it here in Ashford, Colin was right. The opportunities were in New York.

She was going home.

"Hello?" Frankie's voice was followed by a belated knock on the door as she let herself in. "Did you survive Christmas?" she asked. "I saw your car downstairs and figured you called in sick in favor of sleeping in."

"So, you thought you'd wake me up instead?" Rina asked wryly.

"Ha-ha." Frankie sat down on the living room couch, eyeing Rina's laptop. "Are you working from home?" she asked, concerned.

"No. I'm looking for new employment." She shut down the computer and turned toward Frankie. "In fact, you'll probably have a new neighbor soon." At the notion, Rina's stomach twisted with pain and regret.

She didn't want to leave her home here or the friends she'd made. But now that she'd found herself and her calling, she couldn't give up writing and there weren't any other opportunities in the town of Ashford.

"Whoa." Frankie shook her head. "New neighbor? Not a chance. That's like asking me to find a new best friend. Besides, you love it here. So back up and 'splain, Lucy."

Rina rolled her eyes. "You've been watching *I Love*

Lucy reruns again, haven't you?"

Frankie shrugged. "What can I say? It's better than sleeping. Now, quit avoiding the issue and take things from the beginning. Why do you need a new job?"

Rina bunched her hands into fists and explained the paper's financial situation and Colin's means of fixing the problem. "So, you see, the columnists are out, hard news is in. So, I am trying to find a job in Manhattan, where the major national women's magazines are located. My résumé isn't extensive, but this series of five articles is nearly finished and it's the best I've got."

She could fill her résumé with the articles she'd written for her "Hot Stuff" column. She still hoped the paper would run the end of the *Simply Sexy* series, but if not, she'd survive. At least she had an attractive package to show prospective employers.

"Earth to Rina." Frankie waved her hand in front of Rina's eyes. "I asked if you were really just running away from your problems with Colin."

Rina scowled. "I'm made of stronger stuff than that. I'm not running, I'm being smart. There's nothing left for me here, so I'm moving on." But the tight squeeze around her heart made her realize she was lying. There was plenty she wanted here, but she had no way of making those kinds of dreams come true.

"What about Colin?" Frankie asked.

Rina glanced down at her feet before meeting Frankie's gaze. "What about him?"

This time it was Frankie's turn to scowl. "Don't play dumb. It doesn't become you."

Rina let out a groan of frustration and stomped her foot for good measure. She felt a stab of pain in her heel. "Damn."

Frankie put a hand on Rina's shoulder, and at the comforting touch, Rina's eyes filled with tears. The first ones she'd let herself shed. "The man didn't think twice about lying to me, so what's left for me to hang onto now?"

As she spoke, she wanted to believe that the goodness she sensed in Colin wasn't false, that he had regrets despite his agenda. But she didn't know nor could it make any difference. They'd had an affair, by definition a short-term arrangement. She'd always assumed he'd leave, and now, she was going back to New York.

"You can hang onto me, Emma, the friends you made down at the paper, to start with. And I bet Colin would be there, too, if you'd let him."

That was the problem, Rina thought. To listen to him, to hear his side, to let him be there for her—assuming he even wanted to—would leave her vulnerable. No matter how much she loved him, and there was no denying she still did, she didn't think she could open herself up to that kind of hurt again.

She'd lost her husband and now she'd lost Colin. But she'd just now found herself. She couldn't put that on the line. Especially since his departure was imminent if not guaranteed.

COLIN SAT AT his desk, tapping a pencil against the old blotter. He'd never known a woman could make herself so busy she didn't have time for one conversation. Monday, Rina had called in sick. Tuesday, she'd come in, worked on her column, wearing earbuds, no less. When he'd approached her at lunchtime, she'd said she had a meeting and ran out, probably knowing full well he'd be at the hospital all afternoon. Tuesday evening, she hadn't answered her phone, texts or her doorbell, and by Wednesday morning, he was annoyed.

He'd pick her up and carry her over his shoulder and into the back hall if he had to. Today, he wasn't taking no for an answer.

Someone tapping on his shoulder startled him. "What?" he snapped, annoyed, and he whipped around to see Rina.

"A minute of your time, if it isn't too much to ask." She stood before him, one hand on her hip, acting as distant as his latest assignment in South

America.

Now she wanted to talk? "What can I do for you?" he asked, trying to keep things professional in front of the staff despite his earlier thoughts of acting like an irrational caveman.

But outer calm belied his internal struggle. He wanted to take her into his arms and not just apologize but swear he'd make things right. How, he wasn't certain yet. But he damn well would. Even if she never forgave him, he still had to prove he wasn't another man who'd trampled on her needs and desires.

"I spoke to Corinne about this, but she said you're handling personnel now, so I should come to you." Her voice was cold, but her eyes betrayed both pain and what he hoped was a lingering caring beneath the cool veneer.

He wasn't certain where this conversation was headed, but at the word *personnel,* a distinct tingling he'd always referred to as gut instinct set off warning signals in his brain. "About what?" he asked.

"Referrals. I've taken your advice and submitted résumés to some major magazines in New York. Some smaller ones as well." She shook her head in a breezy attempt at looking casual.

She failed, he thought. He saw the wounded woman beneath. But he was nowhere near as confident as he had been when this mess had started, and he wondered if he was only imagining the depth of her hurt. Because if she hurt, it meant she still cared.

She drew a deep breath. "So, if anyone calls, I'd appreciate you giving me a good reference despite all that's gone on between us personally."

At the thought of losing her, fear shot through him. "The hell I will," he said, rising from his seat so he could tower over her.

"Look, Colin, you may not like what I write, but you can't deny I've done a good job. And you can't possibly deny me a decent reference." She clenched and unclenched her fists at her sides.

"Yes, I can." As he'd done once before, he grabbed her hand, ignored the stares, and pulled her out to the hall and into the darkened stairwell.

"You're being unreasonable," she said, backing up against the wall.

He knew better than to press for an advantage or to attempt to get close to her the way he'd done last time. But damn, he wanted to. She wore an oversize white sweater and a pair of jeans that enhanced her curves, making him itch to pull her closer and push their differences aside. If only it was that easy.

"You don't think packing up and sending out résumés is being a bit unreasonable yourself?"

"Did you or did you not plan to get rid of Corinne's columnists?" She bit down on her glossed lips.

He liked the slight insecurity he sensed because it backed up his hunch, that she wasn't as hardened to him as she wanted him to believe. "That *was* my plan."

"So why would you think me preparing for my future is unreasonable?"

"Because between Corinne, Joe, and myself, are going to bring the paper back to life by returning to news, but I still hope to save both columns in the process." He had an afternoon appointment with the accountants and Fortune's together.

The number crunchers didn't like being hassled during the week between Christmas and New Year's, but they'd agreed to meet with him anyway.

She shrugged. "There are no guarantees. So, can I have your word that you'll give me a good recommendation?"

Not the reaction he'd have hoped for, and grabbing a minute to think, he drew a long breath. The dank smell in the hallway assaulted him, waking him up to the bleak reality confronting him. "Rina, I'm truly sorry. You're the last person on earth I'd ever want to hurt. And I'll do everything I can to save your job."

He reached out to graze her cheek, but she turned her head, avoiding his touch. His gut clenched hard.

"You don't get it, do you?" She stared at him wide-eyed. "I'm not hurt or angry because you planned to cut my job. Hard as it is for me to believe, I can understand your need to save the paper, even if it was at my expense." She trembled, wrapping her arms around herself tight. "What I can't understand is how you could lie to me." She pointed to her chest. "After you slept with me, got to know my hopes and dreams, my fears and mistakes, after all that, how could you keep something so important from me?" Her eyes welled up with tears.

Knowing he'd caused them, he wanted to give himself a swift kick. "There was no good way to tell you. I admit, I tried to broach the subject and gauge your reaction a few times."

"At Emma's Christmas party."

He nodded. "We got interrupted by Emma's champagne spill. And by the time I thought I could level with you again, I knew what the column meant to you and why. I realized how devastating the news would be." He wanted to touch her. Instead, he shoved his hands into his back pockets. "If you understand why I did it, can't you forgive me for not telling you?"

She shook her head, and the long ponytail that had grazed his body so lovingly the other night fell over her shoulder.

"I can forgive you, but I can't go back to what we

had." Her voice cracked on her words. "First, you'll leave anyway, and a break is better off clean. Secondly, when I opened up to you, I trusted my instincts, and you proved me wrong."

She let out a laugh that didn't sound funny and his stomach lurched.

"I accept your apology, Colin. But I'm going home to New York." From the look in her eyes, she wasn't joking nor would she be changing her mind. She ducked beneath his arm and headed for the door.

"Rina," he called out.

She turned. For a brief moment, her heart was in her eyes and everything he felt for her, the love, desire, and caring, was obviously reciprocated. Then she schooled her features into a blank mask. One he didn't buy into because he'd seen the feelings beneath.

"What is it?" she asked.

"If I save your job, will you stay? I know you love it here."

She didn't answer.

"Corinne and I will take that as a yes," he said. And then he tossed out his final words. The ones that would be the most difficult for him to live by. "If you do stay, I'll be right beside you. Because my days of running are over." With or without her, Colin knew the time had come to put down roots, accept his family, and live again.

"No, you won't. You'll get bored or feel closed in by some difficult situation. You'll take off like you always do." But she didn't meet his gaze, giving him the hope that she didn't really believe her words.

He had a hunch that deep down she trusted him more than she was letting on. He met her gaze and smiled. "The only way to find out is to stick around yourself."

"Just give me a good recommendation, Colin. Please." Then she walked out the door.

He shook his head and leaned back against the cool wall. What a mess he'd created. Why had he thought he could get involved with Rina and easily walk away?

Because he always had before. Ever since he'd lost both his mother and father, he'd kept his distance from everyone and everything, hoping that he'd never again experience that cavernous feeling of loss. Faced with Rina's withdrawal and threatened departure, he was experiencing it again. And he didn't like it worth a damn. Because this was a loss he didn't think he'd bounce back from. One no amount of running would help.

So he'd better start fighting for what he wanted.

Chapter Twelve

F LOWERS ARRIVED AT Rina's home. A thick, red, luxurious, and obviously expensive bouquet of roses. The card had only two words: *Please stay.*

Next, she checked her e-mail and discovered a card. *Lovers' quarrels are meant to be forgotten,* it said.

And then there was the small box she'd found in her desk drawer. An empty velvet jewelry box. *The best gifts are meant to be given in person. Forgive me.*

The gifts were lovely, all sentimental, all intended to wrap around her heart. But the last one, the empty jewelry box that could only hold a ring, was almost her undoing. Until she reminded herself that none of the presents, the ring box included, could possibly be from Colin. The man had a direct style, and this anonymous note-sending wasn't an approach he'd choose. She couldn't help suspecting somebody else was trying to get her and Colin back together.

The phone rang, distracting her. She picked up the receiver. "Hello?"

"Hi, Rina? It's Cat."

"Cat!" Rina said, glad to hear from the other woman. She loved her outgoing personality and wanted to get to know her better. Then she remembered she wasn't staying in town. A lump rose to her throat.

"I hope you survived the holiday," Cat said. "I know that after a party at my place, I want to crawl into bed and stay there for days. It's amazing how I can cater at other people's homes without any problems, but bring the festivities to my house, and I'm a wreck."

Rina laughed. "I know what you mean. But it was so special having everyone share the holiday with me."

"Even if you did look like you'd lost your best friend?"

Rina blinked. "Emma always said you were perceptive."

"And nosy." A tinkling laughter followed Cat's pronouncement. "Is everything better with you and Colin?"

Rina twirled the phone cord around her finger and leaned back into her comfortable couch. "It's settled," she said. But was it? an inner voice asked.

"Forgive me for prying, but it didn't seem that way to me. Colin came for dinner last night and he was miserable."

Rina's heart pounded in her chest. She didn't want him unhappy, yet she couldn't help the lift in her heart that came with knowing he hadn't gotten over her quickly. Because she was nowhere near over him. "It's not something I caused, Cat."

"Well, I didn't cause my problems with Logan before we got married, but it was up to me to decide I could live with who and what he was." Cat cleared her throat. "Actually, I had to decide I could accept who and what *I* was," she admitted. "But that was me. We're talking about you."

Rina sighed. "Somehow, I'm sensing there's not much difference." Colin accepted her for who and what *she* was. Despite the lies, in her heart, Rina understood that.

She understood that there'd been no honest, graceful way for him to tap her on the shoulder and say, "Hey, Rina, you should know, the paper's in deep financial trouble and the only way out is for me to cut the column you love so much."

Yes, she wished he'd told her. But she understood why he hadn't. She hadn't written advice for women without learning a few things herself. And in the days since discovering the truth, she'd put herself in Colin's position and knew the words couldn't possibly come easily for him. Especially after he'd learned how important her work and newly asserted independence were to her, both missing in her past marriage.

Like Robert, Colin wanted to give her what she desired. Unlike Robert, Colin listened to her needs, accepted them, and didn't want to be the man to destroy her dreams. She sighed.

"Hello?" Catherine called into the phone. "You're breathing but not speaking. What's going on?"

Rina smiled and glanced at the flowers and notes strewn on the table. She didn't want to put Catherine in the middle of her messed-up love life. "Does Colin strike you as a guy who'd send flowers and anonymous notes?"

Cat laughed. "No. Are you receiving them?"

"Yes." Rina paused in thought.

"Emma," they said at the same time.

"That's my guess," Cat said. "You can't imagine the lengths she went to in order to get Logan and I back together. She actually sent me fairy dust!"

Rina rolled her eyes. "That sounds like Emma, all right. Which just goes to show you, even her own social life doesn't keep her busy enough to keep her from meddling."

"Nothing could," Cat said. "Listen, before I forget, the reason I called is that I left my favorite serving dish at your house the other night."

"It's all cleaned for you." Rina drew a deep breath. "How about we meet for lunch sometime next week and I'll return it then?"

Because in her heart, she realized that Ashford was home and she couldn't bear to leave it or the friends she'd begun to make here, regardless of whether Colin decided to stay or go.

"Sounds good."

After agreeing on an exact day and time, Rina hung up the phone and stared around her small apartment. If she closed her eyes, she could see Colin everywhere. He'd made such a big impact in the weekend he'd spent here.

And she missed him now. But how much worse would the ache be if she let things get even more serious and then he took off? She'd lost Robert in an unexpected, devastating tragedy, and she'd promised herself from the beginning that she wouldn't get emotionally involved with Colin because he'd never said he was staying. She didn't want her heart broken again. But control was an illusion and she'd fallen in love despite it all. With a man who would probably leave at the first opportunity, whether he knew it yet or not. His history spoke louder than his words.

She rubbed her aching temples. She didn't know what, if anything, Colin wanted out of their relationship. There was no denying he understood and accepted Rina for who and what she was. The question was did she accept him?

COLIN HAD SPENT a long week gathering information. From the accountants, he'd learned that things were on a slow upswing. From old and loyal advertisers who'd slowly begun to pull out or take less space, he'd discovered that they liked the new offerings but not in place of hard news. The old format, or some semblance thereof, would entice them to advertise more in the hopes of reaching more people again. Especially if Colin promised to stay in town and run things along with Corinne.

And the head guys at Fortune's had latched on to the financial upswing, too. Because of their loyalty to Joe, they'd agreed to ride out the problems for a while longer. The conservative advertiser could live with the risqué quality of the columns, as long as it wasn't shoved in people's faces over breakfast.

From the bank, Colin found out that he qualified for a line of credit, one that would enable him to pay back the lender and leave the fate of the paper solely within Colin's hands. He didn't know why he hadn't thought of it sooner. The line of credit was the only means to convince Rina he had faith in her column, her vision, and in her. It was the only thing he could think of to secure their future. If she bailed on him after that, he couldn't say he hadn't tried.

When his doorbell rang late New Year's Eve, he was surprised since he had no plans and wasn't expecting company. He zipped his jeans, skipping the button. Whoever wanted to talk to him would just have to deal.

He pulled open the door, shocked when he came face-to-face with Rina. He hadn't expected to see her until after the new year and had resigned himself to leaving her alone since that's what she seemed to want. At least until he had his proof compiled and groveling speech ready.

"This is a surprise." He stepped back to let her inside, hoping he wouldn't do something to scare her off before he had a chance to find out what she wanted.

"I had to talk to you, and it wasn't something I could do at work." She bit down on her lower lip. "Can I take off my coat and stay awhile?"

She could stay forever, but he doubted she was ready to hear that. "Sure thing." He helped her off with her jacket and hung it on the rack in the entryway, then gestured for her to head up the stairs.

Following behind, he couldn't keep his eyes off her jean-clad behind, swaying as she walked, and he was hard in an instant. He needed to make her his once more. Not just in a primal male way but in a completely permanent one.

She stood by the couch and turned toward him, a file folder clutched against her chest.

"What do you have there?" he asked.

"Something that I think will simplify your life." She reached inside the manila folder and pulled out a single sheet of white paper. "I know that our relationship complicated your goals, and with Joe sick, you need to do what's right for the *Times,* not for me. So, here."

His stomach in knots, he accepted the paper and skimmed the contents of the letter, his gut cramping more with each word. "You're resigning?"

She nodded, her eyes sad and huge. "You don't need to tiptoe around my feelings anymore or worry about what I'll think of you." She let out a laugh. "Not that I'm saying you worry at all about what I think of you, but I was hoping this would make any decisions easier on you."

"Are you finished?" he asked when she'd stopped rambling.

"Yes."

He held up the paper and ripped it in half. "Don't want it, don't need it. But I do want to know what the hell would possess you to quit a job you obviously love so much."

"All good things must come to an end. And you said yourself, the paper's in financial trouble and getting rid of the newer columnists is the solution."

He raised an eyebrow. "I also remember saying I hoped to save both your job and Emma's."

"Hope isn't definite. And you need to concentrate on what's best for the paper, not what's best for me."

"But you believe I want to save your job?"

One side of her mouth lifted. He'd take the first half-smile in over a week as a positive sign.

"Yeah, I do," she said at last.

"And if I said I had saved your column, that you still had a job, would you stay?"

"Is that a hypothetical question? Because I don't think I can play games anymore."

For the first time, he noticed the stress in her taut expression and the darker circles under her eyes. Well, at least she wasn't getting any more sleep than he was. Reaching out, he grasped her hand. "I'm not looking to play games, either. It's an honest question."

She glanced down at their intertwined hands, his darker skin, her softer, whiter flesh. "I'm staying whether or not there's a place for me at the *Times*," she admitted. "Ashford is home now."

He released a harsh breath. Now *that,* he hadn't expected to hear. "Rina?"

She glanced up to meet his gaze.

"I'm glad."

She blinked, moisture filling her eyes. "You are? Why? Will you stay long enough for it to matter?"

"I told you the other day, I'm not going anywhere. My family is here, my new job is here, and most importantly, you're here."

"Your family's always been here."

He laughed. "Leave it to you to point out the obvious. Yes, my family's always been here, but my heart hasn't been."

She searched his expression, obviously looking deeper inside him. "And now it is?"

He paused, wondering how to explain something he'd only just come to terms with himself. "I needed to face my past in order to have a future. Or at least a stable one, anyway. I've done that now." He squeezed her hand tighter. "Thanks to you. From the day I met you, I recognized you were special. That you had the ability to change me."

Rina's heart felt full. She didn't know whether to laugh because she seemed on the verge of getting everything she wanted or cry because she was so afraid he was saying the words he wanted to believe but wasn't ready to act on. She was still afraid she'd lose him to his emotional fear.

Then again, there was the real possibility it was still her fear she was dealing with, not his. Knowing she had one chance left with Colin, she listened with an open mind, and she hoped with an open heart. "Change you how?" she asked.

"For the better, of course." He winked, then sobered quickly, looking at her with those intense blue eyes she adored. "I never let Joe and Nell inside." He tapped his chest. "I couldn't because I feared it would mean being disloyal to my parents and losing them forever. Of course, they were already gone, but I didn't want to face that. So, I ran. First into a marriage that was doomed from the start because we were so different, and then abroad. But now I've come home and faced the fact that I almost lost Joe. So, I'm through running. I've got too much going for me here."

Rina tipped her head to one side. "Am I included in all that?"

"As long as you've stopped running, too." He gestured to the torn resignation pages that had dropped to the floor. "That was my doing. But you're the one who has to have the courage to stick around. I know you said you're staying, but…"

"Are you calling me a coward?" Rina tried to play things light but the situation was too serious. Too much was at stake, and her joking words fell flat.

Placing an arm around her shoulder, he lowered her to the couch, then met her gaze. "I can't promise you I won't up and die on you, sweetheart," he said, nailing her biggest fear.

Her heart began a rapid, pounding beat and her pulse rate skyrocketed. For the first time since knowing Colin, sexual desire wasn't the cause. Pure adrenaline was. That old fight-or-flight mechanism.

The time had come for her to make a stand. As

Colin had done, she had to face her past and reach out for what she wanted or regret it for the rest of her life. She'd come here intending to bare her feelings, but now, fear lodged in her throat.

But she was letting it go. To move forward, not away. "I can't promise you I won't panic every once in a while," she warned him.

"I can handle a little panic," he said wryly. "In fact, I've gotten used to going out on a limb. I've talked Corinne into taking a second mortgage on their place. And I've co-signed for a loan as well. I've held off the advertisers with a promise of better returns next quarter, and I paid off the guy who lent us money to keep the paper afloat. The only people controlling the *Times* now are me and Corinne. We're running things together." He laughed. "Who'd have thought?"

She blinked, stunned at his news. For one thing, he was working with Corinne, though she shouldn't be surprised. He'd do anything for Joe. Then there was his second bit of news. "You put Joe's place—and your finances—on the line for the paper?"

He shook his head vehemently, shocking her. "I did it for you."

"What?" She wasn't sure she'd heard him correctly.

"I could have continued to use Ron's money and pay off the loan as the we steadily get back on our feet. He was willing. But I don't want you to ever doubt that I have faith in you or your abilities."

Her heart soared higher than it had minutes earlier, strengthening the resolve she'd had all along to risk her heart on this man.

"Colin, I'm sorry. Because I feared another loss, I blamed you for not telling me about the loan, the paper, everything. But that was my problem to resolve, not yours. You never had to prove anything to me." But he cared enough to try, and she loved him even more for it. "And now you've risked so much for me… I don't know what to say."

"I do." He treated her to the endearing, sexy grin she'd missed in the last week.

She leaned closer, waiting.

He stroked her cheek gently. An erotic, tingling sensation shot straight to her belly and a delicious, curling warmth settled inside her.

"You can say you love me, too," he said.

She sucked in a deep breath, then exhaled as everything she'd dreamed of fell squarely into her lap. "You love me?"

"That's what I said."

"In a backhanded way."

"Okay, so call it guy-speak. In female terms, that would be those infamous three words. *I love you.*"

He grinned, but she didn't miss the apprehension in his voice, and she put him out of his misery. "I love you, too."

He met her lips with his in a kiss much needed and long overdue. His tongue swept over her mouth and she opened wide, allowing him inside... and into her heart.

Too soon, he broke the kiss and reached over, pulling open a drawer in the table at the end of the couch. "I left your Christmas party with this still in my jacket. I didn't think I'd get the chance to give it to you." He opened his hand and revealed a bangle bracelet with tiny diamonds embedded in gold.

She sucked in a startled breath. "It's beautiful," she murmured as he snapped it on her wrist.

"I stared at it for many lonely nights, imagining what it would look like on your wrist." He tilted his head and met her gaze. "Merry Christmas, Rina."

"Merry Christmas, Colin." Her eyes misted as she glanced at his beautiful gift.

"What's wrong?"

"I didn't have anything nearly as special for you."

She wrinkled her nose and Colin leaned forward to kiss the tiny lines she'd created. "What'd you get me?"

"Stationery and an engraved pen. It reminded me of the heart of the paper you love so much."

She shrugged, looking so sorry, so lost, and so *his,* Colin didn't care if she'd given him a lump of coal. "Look at it this way. I can use it to write you love notes—every morning for the rest of our lives."

She raised an eyebrow. "Is that a proposal?"

"You're damn right it is." Once again, he reached over and into that drawer, bringing out the second part of her gift, the one he'd bought just yesterday after co-signing the papers for the loan. "Didn't you think that empty jewelry box was a message of some sort?" he asked.

Because he'd left the velvet ring box in her desk, wanting her to find it, wanting her to realize he had it in him to stick around forever.

"*You* gave me the box?" she asked, obviously surprised.

"Of course, I did. Why? Is there another man you think would leave you a private note and personal gift?"

"How about the flowers?" Rina asked.

A jealous tingling ran up his spine. He shook his head. "No flowers."

"Anonymous e-mail?"

"No," he said through clenched teeth.

She smoothed a hand over his cheek. "Relax. Your only competition is an eighty-year-old woman looking to get us back together." She laughed and he was able to calm down.

"Emma didn't," he said with a groan.

"She did."

"Stan's got to take her in hand," he muttered.

"I'd like to see him try. In fact, I'd like to see any man try to tame an independent woman."

"Is that a challenge?" he asked.

A wicked gleam flickered in her gaze. "Are you up to it?"

"Sweetheart, I thought you'd never ask. Step one in taming you." He opened his hand to reveal a diamond ring, then slipped it on her trembling finger. "You now belong to me."

She took in the sign of his love, one thought out and saved for the right moment, and brought it to her chest. A tremor shook her and she shuddered, happiness filling her. "You're so special, Colin. I love you."

He smiled. "I love you, too. Which brings me to step two. You were speechless, then resorted to exalting me. I'd call that tamed. Now, do you need me to bring out the big guns, or do you think I'm up to the challenge?"

Rina loved joking with him, talking with him, sharing, and just being with him. Was he up to the challenge? She moved her hand to the front of his jeans, maneuvering until she cradled his hard length in her palm. "Hmm. I think I need to explore a bit more."

Colin grinned, then lay back on the couch and let her do just that. She unzipped his jeans and pulled them and his boxer briefs down to his ankles, trapping him at her mercy. And with her tongue, she proceeded to show *him* who was in ncharge.

And later, she was more than happy to play the subservient one while he pleasured her. Then they made love, a coming together of equals, Rina thought. A place she didn't mind being for the rest of her life.

Thank you for reading!

Be sure to check out Carly's DARE NATION series starting with DARE TO RESIST.

DARE TO RESIST

He's about to find a baby on his doorstep ... and his assistant in his bed.

Austin Prescott is a lot of things. Ex football player. Sports agent. And as of this morning? Father. Finding a baby on his doorstep should have been a joke but the pink sticky note and baby carrier she came in is deadly serious.

What's an out of his depth bachelor to do? Call his tempting and beyond gorgeous executive assistant and beg her to move in.

Quinnlyn Stone agrees to help Austin until he can straighten out his messy life. It's just another item on her very long To-Do list. It's absolutely not because she's attracted to her very single and extremely handsome boss.

Close quarters. A baby. Undeniable chemistry. What could possibly go wrong?

A complete standalone novel!

✧   ✧   ✧

Did you miss any of the Simply books?

SIMPLY SERIES ORDER:

Simply Sinful

Simply Scandalous

Simply Sensual

Simply Sexy

Don't miss out on the newest info on Carly's books!
Go HERE to join the newsletter and get 2 free books.

www.carlyphillips.com/newsletter

About the Author

NY Times, Wall Street Journal, and USA Today Bestseller, Carly Phillips gives her readers Alphalicious heroes to swoon for and romance to set your heart on fire. She married her college sweetheart and lives in Purchase, NY along with her three crazy dogs: two wheaten terriers and a mutant Havanese, who are featured on her Facebook and Instagram. The author of 50 romance novels, she has raised two incredible daughters who put up with having a mom as a full time writer. Carly's book, The Bachelor, was chosen by Kelly Ripa as a romance club pick and was the first romance on a nationally televised bookclub. Carly loves social media and interacting with her readers. Want to keep up with Carly? Sign up for her newsletter and receive TWO FREE books at www.carlyphillips.com.

Made in the USA
Coppell, TX
01 August 2021